DECAY

FLASHPOINT BOOK 4

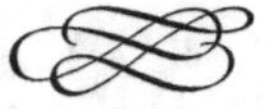

TARA ELLIS

MIKE KRAUS

MUONIC PRESS

DECAY
The Flashpoint Series
Book 4

By
Tara Ellis
Mike Kraus

© 2019 Muonic Press Inc
www.muonic.com

* * *

www.facebook.com/taraellisauthor

* * *

www.MikeKrausBooks.com
hello@mikeKrausBooks.com
www.facebook.com/MikeKrausBooks

CONTENTS

WANT MORE AWESOME BOOKS?

Find more fantastic tales at books.to/readmorepa.

* * *

If you're new to reading Mike Kraus, consider visiting his website at MikeKrausBooks.com and signing up for his free newsletter. You'll receive several free books and a sample of his audiobooks, too, just for signing up, you can unsubscribe at any time and you will receive absolutely *no* spam.

* * *

You can also stay updated on Tara's books by following her Facebook page: www.facebook.com/taraellisauthor

SPECIAL THANKS

Special thanks to my awesome beta team, without whom this book wouldn't be nearly as great.

Thank you!

PREFACE

The art of survival is a complicated tapestry, and the survivors of the flashpoint are learning it's a different pattern for everyone.

It's been two weeks since an extinction-level gamma-ray burst released its fury on the Earth. With the unsuspecting population purged from two-thirds of the planet, those who are left must claw their way back to a semblance of modern civilization. The deadly gamma radiation and massive EMP it produced were enough to cast them into the 1800s and as the days draw into weeks, it's becoming clear that their problems aren't over. In fact, the worst of it might still be looming on the horizon.

Drawn to the town of Mercy for different reasons, a group of refugees have banded together in the middle of the chaos. Tom comes across as your typical cowboy, committed to getting his son, Ethan, home safely to their ranch. As their relationship is challenged in inconceivable ways, the deeper layers of both men are revealed.

Danny isn't from Mercy, and her journey to the small mountain town is driven by the love for her father. A paramedic by trade, the often-underestimated woman has proven she's a fighter. With her companion Sam, and a golden retriever named Grace, they've overcome their own challenges along the way and have teamed up with Tom and Ethan. Together, the ragtag group has pushed ahead and are nearing their destination. Unfortunately, like everything else they've fought for over the past two weeks, nothing comes easy in the new world.

When General Montgomery found himself in charge of not only what was left of the military, but the country itself, he began to drag the pieces back together. In order to do so, he had to make sacrifices. Not everyone has agreed with his tactics, but The Man in the Mountain, sheltered deep inside the Cheyenne bunker in Colorado, is clear on his mission. Armed with the Survivors List, a compilation of people critical to ensuring mankind's survival, the general has brought on the 1st Force Reconnaissance team to collect them.

Led by Master Sergeant James Campbell, the recon unit are the Marines' finest. Highly trained for special ops, they can go where others can't, and that is exactly what the general needs. However, James is a man of honor and when he sees firsthand what has been deemed necessary to ensure the protection of the people, he begins to question General Montgomery's motives.

Mayor Patty has also been burdened with the responsibility of the safety of her own people, the citizens of Mercy. Though full of resourceful and able-bodied individuals, the logistics of keeping over six hundred fed and healthy is nearly impossible. Without the help of a select group, Mercy would fall victim to the same violence besieging the rest of the nation.

Chloe came to Mercy lost and scared, part of a group of troubled teens on a hike that was supposed to improve their outlook on life. While the flashpoint has certainly changed her perspective, the young girl has been able to rise above her hardships and step up as a leader. With her two friends, also troubled teens, and their counselor, Bishop, they have integrated with the people of

Mercy, but still feel a need to continually earn their place among them.

As the environment evolves into a new balance, so do the inhabitants. Russell Boyd has come to Mercy on a mission. Though it isn't quite as noble as the general's, or Mayor Patty.

Russell will help the Earth right its wrongs and he is her weapon of righteousness.

CHAPTER 1

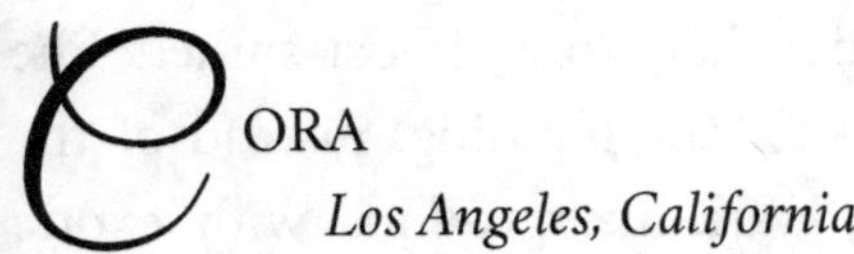

ORA

Los Angeles, California

"GET HER!"

Eleven-year-old Cora cringed at the words and her breath came in ragged gasps as she ran for her life. It was The Crazies. They'd found her.

Her foot slapped into something slick on the pavement and she slid sideways, her thin arms flailing momentarily as she caught her balance. Grunting, Cora threw herself behind a burned-out truck and scrambled over the ground on her hands and knees. Strands of dark hair that escaped her loose braid stuck to her lips, blowing in front of her with each exhalation. Something sharp tore at her bare legs, but she ignored the flash of pain and instead focused on the dark alley only ten feet away.

"Cut her off!" a man shouted. His voice was close by and heavy with the sort of maniacal excitement that had earned the scavengers their name.

The alley. She was in the alley. Momentarily blinded by the deeper darkness, Cora faltered a step and then chastised herself for the hesitation. She had to beat them to the library if there was any chance of escape.

Cora knew The Crazies was a stupid, silly thing to call the men who hunted the streets of Los Angeles. It was the first name that came to mind when she saw them beating a woman on the fifth day after the light thingy happened. Cora prided herself on having a large vocabulary and was a voracious reader, except when she was witnessing horrible things her young brain simply couldn't rationalize.

There!

The eight-story structure loomed tall at the end of the alley and created such a sense of relief that Cora almost smiled. She was approaching from the back of the building, instead of the grand entrance surrounded by park-like grounds with exotic statues and even a pool. Mamma M told her all about the history of the Los Angeles Central Library, and she was the reason Cora had survived so long.

There was a big green dumpster straight ahead, close to the cement wall, and the small girl dared to look back over her shoulder as she sprinted for it. Large, dark shadows were moving across the street behind her, spilling out from the alley. Heavy, ominous pounding announced the approach of The Crazies and Cora knew she wasn't going to make it inside unseen. But she didn't have a choice.

At least once inside the labyrinth of rooms and stacks of books, she stood a chance of staying hidden. Cora was good at hiding. If she remained outside…honestly, she didn't know *what* they'd do to her. They'd certainly take her backpack, filled with her measly score for the day of a bottle of toilet water she'd discovered in an office bathroom, and a granola bar in a desk drawer in the same building.

Then, they would hurt her. Cora had heard others in the library talking about how some groups were resorting to eating each other already. That the odd smell, reminiscent of a barbeque where the pork was cooked too long, wasn't pork. Cora shivered and began to whimper as she rolled the dumpster aside far enough to reveal a service door. She couldn't lock it behind her, because the whole handle had been torn out days before. That was how she was able to use it.

Certain that rough hands were about to grab her at any moment, Cora squeezed through the door and stumbled down the three cement steps on the other side. The clatter of the metal cart being manhandled echoed into the passageway behind her and as she ducked into a side hall, the outer door slammed open.

"Come on, little kitten!" mocked the same man who had yelled before. "You can't hide from us."

Removing her dirty sandals, Cora began to tiptoe through the service hallway as fast and as silently as possible, while the group of men pursuing her made no effort to be quiet. That's what she was counting on.

A light snapped on, and a beam cut through the thick darkness of the windowless hallways. Cora gasped at the unexpected sight and then slapped a hand over her mouth to try and smother the sound. The light bobbed and the footsteps quickened as they ran. They'd heard her.

Cora blinked, battling her tears of fear and frustration. She did her best to ignore the sounds of pursuit and focused on her goal.

Turn right here...

"Here, kitty, kitty!"

Now, turn left...

Shadows moved grotesquely in the dancing light as the men closed in on her, and Cora used her terror to push her legs faster than they'd ever moved before. Even if it had been daylight, that area of the building had no windows and was perpetually in a state of darkness. Normally, she would light her stub of a candle, but had to instead rely on the dozens of times she'd walked the route, running her hands down the wall to help guide her.

There! Cora gasped again, this time in relief, as she came to a dead end and her hand wrapped around the handle of the only door. Opening it, she was greeted by the flickering light of several candles.

The main room of the library was called the rotunda, according to Momma M, who had worked there for over ten years. Cora met the woman there the day after her life was destroyed. The day her mom was killed because she'd been a brat.

When Cora had found out she wouldn't be able to attend football camp with her two best friends because girls weren't allowed, she'd pouted for two weeks. It was only after her mom promised to take her to Disneyland that she'd smiled again, and *that* was how they'd ended up in LA that day. It was all her fault.

Cora knew that wasn't true, but it didn't matter. When she was alone in the dark, replaying the day she watched her mother die over and over again…it was the only phrase that echoed in her mind. *It was her fault.*

They'd been on a tour bus, going through downtown Los Angeles on their way to Hollywood. Cora had been shocked and dismayed at most of the highlights of the tour and opted not to get off the bus, out of fear. The only building she wanted to see was the Central Library. They passed it at one point and she'd bobbed up and down in her seat, only to watch it recede out the back window. Getting up for a better view of it as they drove away was what ended up saving her life.

There'd been an odd, whitish light that washed out the sun and made everything look brighter than it really was. Then, the bus died. Cora had turned back to where her mom was still seated, in the middle of the bus, with the intention of complaining about yet one more thing. As their eyes met, another bus slammed into them. Cora figured her mom died right away, based on what she looked like afterward. She'd read that was supposed to help with grief, but it didn't. It couldn't erase any of it from her mind, or change the fact that she would never see her mom again.

When no one came to help even though she'd sat with her mom's body for hours, Cora did the only thing she could think of doing. She went to the library. She was able to see it still, even through all the smoke. By then it was getting dark and people were already rioting and looting. Fires raged in too many buildings to count, but not the library, and that was all that mattered to Cora.

"Hey!"

Cora's head snapped up, slamming her back to the present, as she sought out the source of the warning shout. A woman with long black hair was standing near the main check-out desk, holding a bat. Shrinking back, Cora veered away from the lady. However, the woman continued to shake the bat and it wasn't directed at Cora.

"You can't be here!" she screamed, pointing the bat at someone across the room.

Cora turned to see four men running into the rotunda, each of them clasping a different weapon. She guessed that the man in front, holding a large machete, was the one who'd been taunting her. She smiled. Her plan might already be working.

There were at least three different groups of survivors living in the central library. While they weren't as bad as The Crazies and didn't make people disappear, they still used force to take what they wanted. Cora knew that based on what she'd seen and heard. Since she wasn't sure who could be trusted, she avoided all of them. It was safer that way.

The rotunda was an immense, three-story tall room with

domed mosaic ceilings. The marble floor added an air of regality to the intricate architecture, so that it looked and felt more like a cathedral than a library. In the daylight, something called the zodiac chandelier was visible and featured a glass Earth that hung suspended above them all.

As Cora scooted in between a row of books, she glanced up at the murky ceiling, and thought fleetingly of how it was an accurate representation of the darkness the planet was now suffering in.

Other voices joined the argument, and Cora took advantage of the distraction by dashing behind the main counter. That was where she'd first encountered Momma M, a large black woman with an incredibly sharp mind and huge heart. She knew everything about the library, and Los Angeles. She'd taken Cora in and made sure she had enough food and water for several days. Momma M was also the one who had shown Cora how to disappear into the walls.

Kneeling down, Cora pulled at an ornate, metal grate that was situated low on the back wall. It revealed a small opening less than two by two feet. It was big enough for her, though, and Cora slid in feet first so she could pull the grate into place behind her.

Once inside, she wiggled backwards on her stomach, the cement cold against her bare skin as her T-shirt snaked up. Cora wasn't sure what exactly the passageways were originally used for. Maybe heating or something equally boring, but she'd come up with an incredible tale involving fairies, evil trolls, and a handsome prince. She was the princess, of course, and like any good story, she would be rescued at the end.

Cora choked back a sob as she clung to the belief that she would be found. That her dad, from their home in Texas, would somehow find her there, hidden in the walls of the Los Angeles Central Library, and whisk her back home.

Her feet lost their purchase and then hung in midair momentarily as Cora reached her goal, some thirty feet back from the entrance. Pushing harder, her knees moved out into the open space, and then she was hanging, suspended over what could have been a hundred or ten feet, but in reality was only five.

Cora dropped down and landed in a crouch, holding her breath for a moment in the pitch blackness to make sure there wasn't any other movement. When all she heard was the escalating argument echoing in the distance, she closed her eyes and took one long, deep breath.

Slowly removing her backpack, Cora then dug a lighter out of her back pocket and felt around in the darkness for a candle. After lighting one, she hesitated and then lit a second. It had been a bad night.

Cora's "room" was some sort of central connecting hub for the network of small tunnels. The space itself wasn't more than five feet across and octagonal. She had lined the walls with books, and covered the floor with a motley collection of blankets, pillows, and a couple of small couch cushions from the reading room. One section of the wall was left bare, where Cora was keeping track of the days by making marks on the cement with a piece of chalk she'd found.

She had started doing that on the second day Momma M didn't come back. The older woman went to do some scavenging, because she said there wasn't any more water left in the pipes. Cora understood that they couldn't live more than a few days without water, but they had both seen the violence that raged through the city and it scared her. She had begged Momma M not to go without her, but the kind woman wouldn't allow it.

The tour guide on the bus two weeks before had talked nonstop. Cora remembered three things he'd said: the city of Los Angeles was over five hundred square miles, had more than four million people in it, and was bigger than New York.

Cora tried to get to the ocean. She had another fantasy about living on the beach and surviving off the land, like *The Swiss Family Robinson*. Unfortunately, the only jungle Cora managed to see was concrete. Even though she'd left early in the morning, she ended up getting caught out in the dark. The reality was that she had no idea which direction to go, or for how long. She was lost.

Sighing, Cora grabbed her chalk and made another line on the wall. Fourteen days since the end of the world. Sitting down on one of the cushions, she pulled her *Frozen*-themed backpack into her lap and stared longingly at the smiling girl in the image. Closing her eyes, she envisioned herself high up in a castle turret, deep in the woods of a medieval forest.

Soon.

Her prince would come and rescue her.

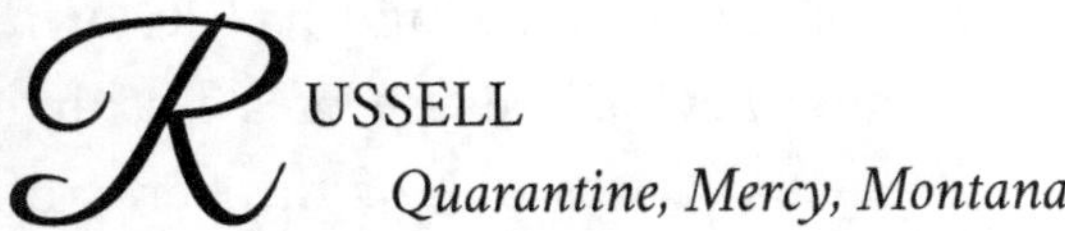

CHAPTER 2

USSELL

Quarantine, Mercy, Montana

"I THOUGHT WE SHOULD MEET, Father Rogers."

Russell did his best to appear meek as he sized up the woman seated across from him. Mayor Patty Woods was formidable. That much was immediately apparent. She looked to be in her sixties, of average size, with her graying hair pulled up tight and neat. Her nails were trimmed but not painted. She wore little makeup, if any, other than some eyeliner and lip gloss. She sat with her hands folded on the table, leaning forward slightly; a position that, while reserved, welcomed conversation. Russell knew exactly how to handle the mayor.

"Especially in light of how you came to be in Mercy," Mayor Patty continued. "Jed returned a short time ago from his run and confirmed your encounter, so I also wanted to thank you, in addition to introducing myself."

Russell took care to also lean in to show interest, except that he opened his arms in an inviting manner and placed his hands palms-down on the table. "Please, Madam Mayor, call me Russell. It's a pleasure to meet you, and helping Jed was something I'm sure anyone in my position would have done."

The mayor didn't move, nor did she comment on his bravery. Russell resisted the urge to frown. The conversation itself was unexpected since he wouldn't be out of quarantine for another nine hours. That was when his twenty-four hours of isolation would be up. He glanced at the finger paintings that adorned the walls surrounding them and did his best not to cringe. The town had converted the small school building into a clinic, and the kindergarten room was their quarantine area. According to the young man who'd escorted him there a day ago, it was because the room was on the far end of the building, and had its own separate bathrooms. Funny, how having the use of a flushing toilet made one feel human again. It was one of the perks of living in a small town; everything was on a septic system. All you needed was a bucket of water next to the toilet to keep things moving.

The silence had drawn out to the point of being awkward so Russell gave the mayor a quizzical look.

"Jed said you never mentioned being a pastor." While Mayor Patty's tone wasn't accusatory, neither was it friendly.

Russell had been expecting the question. He took a moment to sigh heavily while looking down at his hands, his shoulders slumping. When he looked back up at the mayor, he offered her his most charming smile, knowing the effect it had on most women. "Mayor, can I be honest with you?"

Sliding her hands back across the table, the older woman allowed them to fall into her lap as she leaned back in her seat and relaxed slightly, her demeanor changing. "Let's both drop the formalities. Call me Patty. And I've always preferred the truth."

"Well...Patty, the reason I didn't talk with Jed about my role as a pastor is because I'm not certain I deserve that title anymore. I—" Russell turned away from Patty then, his handsome face contorted with pain and strife. "I've seen things, turned a blind eye to atrocities, and the truth is that I'm questioning my faith. I'm not sure I can get it back." He let out a slow breath and discreetly wiped away a tear.

Patty reached out and placed a comforting hand on top of Russell's and he knew he had her. He responded by hanging his head further, submitting himself to her platitudes.

"I've had my faith challenged several times during my life," Patty offered, her voice kind. "While it all pales in comparison to what's happening now, it still comes down to what we *do* with it. Questioning our faith is a normal, human reaction. Allowing it to help you grow and solidify your beliefs is the challenge. Otherwise, it *will* destroy it."

Russell placed his other hand on Patty's and gave it a quick squeeze before pulling away. Nodding his head, he took an audible breath and then rubbed his hands together. "You're a wise woman, Patty. Perhaps you should lead the church body, as well as the town."

"Gracious, no!" Patty retorted, blushing slightly. "I'm having a hard enough time as it is. I'm certainly not qualified to be responsible for anyone's soul." Patty eyed Russell for a moment and seemed to come to a decision. "You know, a good method for rediscovering one's faith is to become submerged in it."

Russell steepled his fingers and raised them to his lips while squinting at Patty. He already knew where she was headed and wasn't surprised at the ease with which he'd manipulated her. It really didn't take much with most people, although he had to admit to a slight surge of disappointment. He'd hoped she might prove to be more of a challenge. "What are you suggesting?" he asked with false trepidation.

"Father White has been leading Mercy down the road to

righteousness for more than thirty years. Although he's an amazing priest who has scared many a child into submission with his sermons, the flashpoint took a toll on his health."

"Radiation?" Russell guessed, eyebrows raised.

"Unfortunately," Patty confirmed. "Father White is over eighty years old and became quite ill. He's still struggling and I… we all worry about how hard he's pushing himself. I think it would be a welcome relief for him to have some help."

Russell shifted in his chair and looked up at the Mickey Mouse clock on the wall, although it of course didn't work. Doing his best to appear uncomfortable he cleared his throat before answering. "You've been more than kind, and to offer me a chance to explore my convictions is—well, extremely gracious. How can I say no?"

Patty smiled, and Russell was intrigued, as always, by the course of human nature. They were essentially creatures forever looking for approval, which then equated to a false sense of love and acceptance. It was extremely liberating once you didn't constrain yourself with those needs.

"I spoke with Tim's parents," Patty said, and Russell's interest was once again piqued. "They said they never heard of you."

Russell's smile was genuine as he prepared his scripted response. He was rather enjoying the conversation now. "I'm not at all surprised to hear that. Tim said they weren't churchgoers and had in fact had a falling out with him a couple of years ago over religion. I doubt bringing up his Episcopal priest friend would have been a warm topic of conversation."

Patty chuckled. "That sounds like the Ridgeways. They always make sure I keep a strict delineation between church and state. I once had Father White open a city hall meeting with prayer and I was lectured on it at every opportunity by Mr. Ridgeway for over a month." Her smile faded and she became serious again. "They're devastated, of course, to hear about Tim, but are grateful to you for bringing them the information."

"I first met Tim over a year ago," Russell lied. Leaning back in the chair again, he became thoughtful while staring out a nearby window. The steep mountains of the valley were visible in the distance, reminding him of where he was. He had reached his goal and needed to solidify his place in Mercy. Over the next few days he'd be laying the foundation, and it all began with a solid story of his past.

"I went to the asylum where Tim worked as a guard, to give communion to the residents," Russell explained, looking back at Patty. "He attended the service and stayed afterward to speak with me. It was the beginning of an unexpected friendship. He soon began going to my small church in town and we often went fishing afterward, on Sunday afternoons. Tim reminded me of my younger brother," Russell said, which wasn't a complete false-hood. "He was kindhearted and treated all of the residents under his care with empathy and compassion. I only wish I was the one who had been shot that night, instead of him. There wasn't anything I could do."

Patty made a clucking sound and patted his hand again. "No one blames you, Father. I mean, Russell. It's a miracle that you made it this far." Standing, Patty went to a bottle of hand sanitizer and saturated her hands. "It's already obvious that you're not ill, but I hope you understand we still have to take these precautions."

"Completely understandable," Russell answered, impressed with how priestly he already sounded.

Patty hesitated at the door and then looked back at him. Her eyes were glossy and her lips quivered. He was impressed that after all of the death and extremes Patty experienced, she was still able to show such emotion. "Tim was a good man," she said shakily. "I knew him since he was a boy. Though I'm sad to learn he didn't make it, there's some comfort in knowing that his soul was at peace."

Russell thought about those final moments as Tim writhed on top of him, clawing at his arms…the scuff marks on the floor. He watched as the door closed shut behind Mayor Patty, and then allowed a sneer to transform his handsome features into something vile.

"Peace isn't what I have to offer."

CHAPTER 3

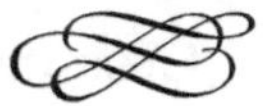

ATTY

Mercy, Montana

"FATHER, I thought you'd welcome the help!" Patty stood with her hands on her hips, facing the stubborn old man. "The church apartment hasn't been used in years. It seems like the perfect solution to getting the help you've been asking for."

Father White waved a hand at Patty before turning away from her in annoyance. He shuffled back up the sidewalk, toward the church. It was an antiquated building, exactly what someone would expect to see in a small-town setting: white clapboard siding, large ornate stained-glass windows, wide-sweeping steps, and even a bell tower.

While the Catholic clergyman had always taken great pride in his church and large congregation, Patty never thought he'd be so stingy about sharing it. "Father!" she called to his back, genuinely shocked by his behavior. "You won't even talk to me about it?"

Huffing loudly, Father White stopped and turned back

abruptly, tugging at his robes as he did so. Patty noticed he'd taken to wearing the formal attire all the time, rather than strictly during services, like he used to. She considered the very real possibility that the older man had been pushed past his limits both physically and emotionally. The thought was disturbing and also saddening. While he could be ornery, the pastor had been a staple of Mercy for as long as she could remember.

"The man left his flock." Crossing his arms over his chest, Pastor White seemed to be challenging Patty to deny it.

Patty blinked, taken aback. *That* was why he was in a huff? "My understanding is that his church burned down, father. What else was he supposed to do?"

"The congregation is the body of the church, not the building," Father White said stiffly. "He abandoned his parishioners."

Patty studied the man's face for a moment, taking in the deep lines and blue eyes that still sparkled with intelligence. She knew he had a kind heart, which was why his reaction was so unexpected. However, she had to acknowledge that he might have a valid point. "Father, we've been extremely blessed here in Mercy. We've been protected from the worst of what's happening to the rest of the world. I understand your concern, I just think it's the sort of question you should be asking Father Rogers yourself, instead of judging him."

The remark had the desired effect as Father White flinched in acknowledgement of the accurate statement. He cleared his throat and squinted up at the clouds building on the far edge of the valley. "He's still in quarantine."

Patty nearly failed to stifle the laugh that threatened to escape. "He'll be out in time for the barbeque later tonight, Father. Perhaps that would be a good opportunity for you to meet him. You know, he did travel over five hundred miles to reach Mercy, just so he could let Mr. and Mrs. Ridgeway know about Tim, who was a part of his congregation."

Father White grunted in response, but didn't say no. It was progress.

"Three days," Patty said, reaching out to rest a hand on the older man's arm. "That's all I'm asking, Father. Allow Pastor Rogers to stay at the church for three days, and if, at the end of that time, you still think it's a bad idea, I'll find different accommodations for him."

The distinct jangling of tack and wagon parts caused both Patty and Father White to turn toward the road. Sure enough, Caleb and Tane were seated atop the old wagon, headed their way. Patty knew she was going to lose her chance to get him to agree, so she looked over at the pastor and purposely crossed her arms and raised her eyebrows. "So? Do we have a deal?"

Throwing both of his hands up in defeat, Father White began to shuffle away again. "Three days, and not a minute longer," he said over his shoulder.

"What's that grin for?" Caleb asked as he pulled the wagon to a stop a few feet away.

Patty's smile widened in response to her husband's question. "Oh, just a little PR. What are you two up to?" She asked, turning her focus onto Tane. Mr. Latu wasn't well known to Patty, but he'd been spending a lot of time with Caleb ever since they began work on the radios. The Pacific Islander was one of the biggest men Patty had ever seen and the combination of his calm demeanor and inviting dark eyes intrigued her. He moved to Mercy three years prior and according to Caleb, had a daughter who lived in Helena but had been out of town during the flashpoint.

"Bishop spent all morning refining the filtration system on the spring," Tane explained. He gestured at the large green plastic water tank in the back of the wagon. It had been an incredible find, tucked away in a barn at one of the farms. It held five hundred gallons and was originally meant for watering cattle. It would have been impossible to move it around without the wagon, and they weren't even sure the cart could handle the weight until the first, nerve-wracking trip.

Tane slapped the side of the tank. "He's improved the flow so that it's nearly twice as much. Once we work out the hiccups on filling and delivering it, we estimate at least a thousand gallons a day is possible."

"When can we start filling the reserve tank?" Patty asked. She saw Tane's smile falter and realized she'd done it again…failed to recognize an accomplishment while reaching for a further goal. "This is amazing!" she rushed to add. "I'm just eager to see some drinking water in the main holding tank." The five-thousand-gallon tank had been dragged down, literally, from the useless water-treatment plant. It was their goal to have it filled by winter. Even then, it would only be enough to supply the town's population for five days, if something happened to the spring.

"Understandable," Tane replied, nodding in agreement.

"We're on our way to drop this off at the water center," Caleb explained the obvious. He was referring to what used to be the coffee stand and its adjacent parking lot, located at the south end of town. It was a good, central location with plenty of open space for setting up the necessary water stations, as well as the holding tank. "We'll exchange this clean water for the five-gallon river water barrels so the teens can make their house-check in quadrant one."

"Did quadrant four get completed yesterday?" Patty asked, realizing she'd been neglecting to check in with the extremely important task force. The past two days had been a whirlwind of activity involving the butchering of Sandy's steer, organizing the town dinner, and getting a solid start on the farmer's market.

"I believe Betty took quadrant four's notebook up to your office this morning," Caleb replied, looking concerned. "Haven't you been to your office yet? It's nearly noon."

Patty felt disoriented for a moment and looked around fleetingly to locate the sun. How could it be so late? She hadn't even had breakfast yet, let alone lunch. She should have never gotten sidetracked with the newcomer, but the Ridgeways somehow heard about Tim and the mysterious pastor, and she couldn't avoid the conversation any more when they stopped her that morning on her way into town.

If she dug a little deeper, Patty might have to admit that she was also avoiding the house-check task force. It was headed up by Gary, whom she'd been dodging for the past two days. However, Councilman Paul, their old mayor Ned, and Councilwoman Betty were a part of the group, so there was really no excuse. Patty simply had too much on her plate.

Rubbing at her forehead in a futile attempt to stop a mounting headache, Patty figured it was more of a platter, when she added Bishop to the growing list of people to evade. Caleb didn't seem to think there was anything unusual about his interest in the radio and it was hard for Patty to convey why she'd found the situation odd. Bishop was the golden boy *and* she'd been the one to allow him to stay in spite of Paul's protests. With everything that was going on, it wasn't in anyone's best interest to say or do anything to cast doubt on Bishop, and thereby her judgement.

Giving up on stopping the pain in her head, she dropped her arm in defeat. "I'm headed to my office now," Patty said to her husband while glancing up at him and hoping he didn't pick up on the weariness in her voice. "I'll go through the requests and organize a response this afternoon."

The system was rather ingenious, Patty had to give that much credit to Paul. There were a hundred and sixty-eight houses on the outskirts of Mercy. While the bulk of them were located in close proximity to the main area of the town, quite a few were spread out further into the valley. Fortunately, the most remote homes were working farms and belonged to people who could manage better on their own than any organized group could pretend to do. That left a grid of four sections, each with roughly thirty houses per quadrant.

Paul put together his task force and they spent several days creating detailed notebooks, one for each quadrant. Each house had a section within the notebook, and that was how they tracked each home on a weekly basis, for their health, wants, and needs. It had been Betty's idea to use the high school kids. She was a teacher and knew all of the teens and their families, and believed it was the perfect way to put them to work.

They ended up with a dozen kids, overseen by the four adults, working together to closely monitor the residents of Mercy. The house-check task force was separate from the drinking water delivery, but they did offer river water, or what was lovingly referred to as "The Flush".

Since Mercy didn't have a central sewer system, everyone was on septic. Because of that, so long as they had a source of water to pour into the bowl, they could continue flushing. It was one of the things Patty hadn't thought of, when discussing disaster scenarios in the past, and it had turned out to be extremely important. When it came to sanitation and keeping people healthy, having human feces piling up was something to be avoided at all costs.

That was why making sure everyone had working toilets was part of the house-check task forces duties. The first week proved to be more than the teens could handle, and extra help was needed to get some toilets functioning again. Not everyone had the means to get out and carry the necessary water, so several homes were pretty nasty.

The church bell began to toll, marking the noon hour, and Patty jumped so high she nearly fell over. How Father White still managed to get up to the bell tower and pull that rope was a mystery. Laughing at herself, she went through the practiced gesture of smoothing down her hair to prove she was still in control. As the last gong faded, she moved toward the wagon. "Mind if I catch a ride with you?"

Instead of reaching out a hand to help Patty up, Caleb surprised her by jumping down next to her. Encircling her in his strong arms, he pulled her in close. "I worry about you, Patty," he said into her hair. "You look so tired."

Patty drew back and cupped her husband's face with her hands, drawing on his strength. "I can't remember a time when I wasn't."

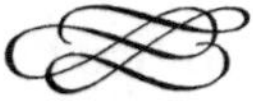

CHAPTER 4

Tom

Near Grahams Place, Montana

TOM RESISTED the urge to yell at Ethan to slow down. He knew his son was capable of managing his own horse, and it probably wasn't a bad idea to give the spirited gelding his own head every once in a while. Tom had gone out of his way the past two days to treat Ethan like more of an adult, especially in light of how he'd managed to orchestrate their release from the shelter.

Thanks to a forestry road Ethan's Army friend told them about, they'd been able to shave several miles off their trip home by cutting east over to Montana Highway 87. After camping next to a lake the night before, their group now headed north again. Tom wasn't as familiar with the region, although once they crossed Interstate 90, he'd know exactly where they were. From there, they were in the homestretch.

"It's gorgeous out here," Danny said as her horse trotted up next to Tom. "I don't know why I've never been down this way before. I guess I was always too busy."

Tom eyed Danny with some uncertainty. It wasn't like her to make small talk. He'd come to accept the obvious fact several days ago that she didn't like being around him. Not that he could blame her, after their initial encounter and his subsequent behavior at the FEMA camp. But something almost imperceptible had shifted over the past twenty-four hours. Since leaving the shelter, Danny was making more eye contact with him, was including him in conversations, and now...making small talk. Unless he was imagining it all, which was entirely possible.

"You've got that thousand-yard stare again," Danny teased, narrowing her eyes at him. "I can't decide if you're still suffering from some concussion symptoms, or if you're just a very serious guy with some deep layers."

Chuckling, Tom removed his cowboy hat and ran his other hand through his thick, dark hair. "I'm going to have to go with the concussion theory," he said, smiling back at her. Their eyes met briefly and there was something about the way she looked at him, the cool intelligence that made it clear he wasn't fooling her.

Replacing his hat, Tom focused on the road ahead of them before gesturing up at the mountains to their west. "I think those are part of the Horn Mountain range," he explained, choosing to reply to her original comment and avoiding any discussion about his "layers". "It means we must be back in Montana."

"We weren't before?" Danny asked, looking amused.

Tom shifted in his saddle. "On that last part of the forest road and lake, we dipped back into Idaho."

"Oh," Danny replied, eyeing him again. "I guess I need to spend more time looking at the maps with you and Sam at night. I haven't wanted to interrupt your man time."

Tom looked over at her questioningly and saw that she was teasing him again. Knowing there was no way to back out of the bait she set, he changed the subject. "So, what made you decide to become a firefighter?"

Danny's brows drew together and she screwed her nose up at him. "Most people ask me about my choice to be a paramedic."

Feeling on more solid footing with the conversation, Tom shrugged his broad shoulders before smiling at her. "I figure I already know the answer to that. I'm much more intrigued with what motivates you to put on bunker gear and drag heavy equipment around."

Danny rolled her eyes. "Don't tell me you're one of those good ol' boys who's shocked anytime he meets a woman who can do a man's job as well as a man."

Tom couldn't help it—he chortled first and then burst out into full laughter. When he saw Danny getting red in the face, he put his hands out to placate her. "I keep forgetting, you obviously haven't met my mother. She single-handedly ran our ranch for a year after Dad died, and I was raised watching her do things some men can't. She's the one who taught me how to fish *and* how to hunt."

"Oh," Danny said quietly, clearly intrigued by the unexpected reaction.

Tom leaned forward against his saddle horn and tipped his hat up so she was sure to see his face and know he was being sincere. "I have the same level of respect for anyone who can step up and get things done when they need to, be they a man *or* a woman."

Danny smiled then, and the way it transformed her face made his breath catch. "Honestly, the only reason I ever became a firefighter was because I had to in order to get my paramedic training. In our county, emergency services are fire-based, so you can't be a medic without first being a firefighter. I specifically got hired on with our department so they'd put me through the classes and get me my certification. But you know what? The first time I put that bunker gear on and started playing with fire, I was hooked. If I could have stopped being a paramedic and stuck to just the fire side of business, I might—" Her voice trailed off and Danny got a faraway look.

"You might what?" Tom pressed, interested in hearing more of her story.

Wiping at her nose, Danny sat up straight and gave her head a shake. "Never mind. A conversation for another time. Preferably over a fire and a beer."

It was Tom's turn to smile. "Unless my mom pillaged the stash, I might be able to arrange that in a few days."

Grace interrupted their discussion with a string of high-pitched barks. It didn't sound normal and they both pulled their horses to a stop, alarmed.

"Something's wrong," Danny said, straining to see where the barking was coming from.

Tom also searched for the source, which was somewhere up ahead of them. Sam's horse had chased after Tango, leaving Danny and Tom to trail behind. He chastised himself for allowing them to get so spread out. They needed to be more careful, especially on the steep, wooded roads where visibility wasn't very far.

They'd only encountered a handful of people since leaving the shelter and most of them simply kept to themselves. One woman had happily greeted them and eventually traded a dozen fresh eggs for a mac and cheese MRE. Tucked away in the mountains it was easy to forget what was happening, but given their recent stay with the US government, Tom couldn't accept any excuses. He knew better than to get so distracted.

"Grace!" he shouted, spurring Lily into a gallop. "Ethan!" his voice echoed through the valley and mixed with Grace's continued barking. Underlying it was another new sound, that caused Tom to break his horse into a run.

Other riders, coming through the trees from either side. All he could think about was Ethan and that he'd let him out of his sight. "Ethan!" he yelled again, and this time he heard a reply.

Rounding a bend in the road, Tom first saw Grace bounding toward him, with Ethan and Sam several hundred feet farther away. They were stopped, and Ethan was pointing to the woods, having also heard the approaching horses.

Tom sat up from his crouch and Lily slowed in response. Removing his hat, he lifted it up in the air and waved his arm in a broad circle before pointing it at Ethan and Sam. His son didn't need any further encouragement, and he turned Tango back around and took off with Sam close behind.

Looking over his shoulder, Tom saw that Danny was struggling to catch up with him. While she was a quick learner and took well to riding, running on pavement with a horse that didn't have a smooth gait wasn't easy. "Come on!" he called out, although he knew it wasn't necessary.

As Danny got close, Tom saw movement from the trees behind them. It hadn't been more than a few minutes since he first heard them, and the other horses were already on top of them. It was an ambush, and he should have seen it coming.

Danny shot past him, her eyes wide with fear as she fought to stay in the saddle. As Tom turned to follow, he saw two horses lunge out onto the road, the men on their backs hooting as dirt and debris was kicked into the road. They were dressed in rags and covered in filth, looking wild and desperate.

"Ha!" one of the men shouted, urging his horse on as two more riders exploded from the other side of the road.

Tom saw that they were gaining on the pack horse, and while losing it would be a huge blow, they'd be okay. It was only a few more days' ride to Mercy and they could get along without the supplies. Tom reached for the gun strapped to his leg and turned slightly to peer over his shoulder and get a better view. If he could present a harder target than they thought, while leaving the pack horse behind for the easy picking, there was a chance they'd settle for it and let them go.

Drawing the 1911 from the holster, Tom debated on how to use the last bullet. Everything slowed down as his adrenaline surged and his heart raced. The pack horse fell behind him and then Danny appeared on his right as Lily caught up to the slower horse. He avoided looking at her and instead concentrated on the men, who were quickly gaining on them. The one in the lead had a rifle and he was bringing it around to line up a shot at Tom.

Tom reacted first, and his gun roared as the shot struck the rider high on the chest. The rifle retorted a second later, but the man was already falling backward, causing his round to go wide.

The noise was enough to prompt Danny's horse to go faster as she clung to anything she could find purchase on. Tom willed her to hold on as he watched her struggle, knowing that if she fell, they were doomed. While it would be enough of a distraction to allow Ethan and Sam to get away, he would do everything he could to prevent them from taking Danny. Tom felt for the large hunting knife strapped to his other leg, reassuring himself that it was there.

The sound of the pursuit didn't lag, and Tom dared another look, certain it would be met with a bullet. The three remaining riders had passed the pack horse, ignoring it to continue the chase. The fourth man was stopped some distance back, slumped over in his saddle, nursing his wound. Tom didn't see any other rifles and the three bandits that were left appeared intent on simply catching them. Based on the maniacal smiles he could see, it didn't seem like much of an alternative to being shot.

Just when Tom thought they might be able to put up a decent fight, two more riders appeared on the road ahead of them. Of course, a proper ambush meant cutting off their escape.

He couldn't tell if the new attackers had guns, but it really didn't make a difference. "Charge them!" he shouted to Danny, and he could see her nodding in agreement.

When they were still a hundred feet away, seven other horses came careening down the road, causing the two new bandits to turn and look. At first, Tom thought it might have been Ethan and Sam but it was immediately obvious that this was an entirely different group, dressed in leather and all heavily armed.

"What the—" Danny cried out as her horse balked. At the limit of her abilities, Danny was thrown sideways and then fell, grunting in pain as she hit the pavement.

Tom leaped from Lily's back before she'd come to a stop and stood over Danny, knife in hand. Arms out, he turned first to his left, and then his right, trying to gauge where the first strike would come from.

To his shock, the new band of riders were continuing their charge, straight for the second group of bandits. The three initial attackers turned around, and Tom realized that they were running *away* from the leather-clad men. It was then that several shots rang out and Tom ducked instinctively, covering his head. It proved to be unnecessary, as the bullets hit the ground harmlessly in the wake of the retreating riders.

The silence following the melee was deafening, and Tom was acutely aware of Danny's ragged breathing from behind him as he scrutinized one of their apparent rescuers dismount. He was a large man, and walked like someone who was used to being in charge. Tom blindly put a hand out to help Danny to her feet, while watching him approach.

Stopping at a safe distance, the older man narrowed his eyes as he stared at Tom. His face was deeply lined, and he sported a full beard and moustache. His cowboy hat was clean but well-worn, as were his leather chaps and gloves. Tom knew a rancher when he saw one and he was instantly at ease.

Relaxing his stance, Tom re-sheathed the knife he'd still been clasping and then offered his empty hand. "Name's Thomas Miller, owner of Miller Ranch up in Mercy."

The lines around his eyes deepened as the man smiled in response. Taking several steps forward, he took Tom's hand in a firm grip. "Pleasure to meet ya, Mr. Miller. I'm Jesper Duke. Welcome to Graham County."

CHAPTER 5

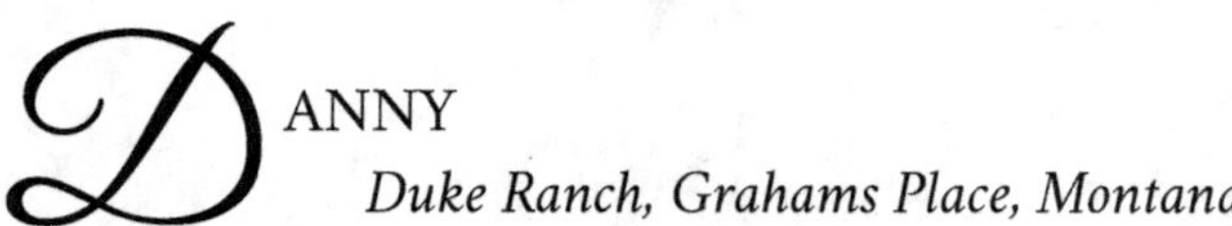

D ANNY
Duke Ranch, Grahams Place, Montana

"W HAT EXACTLY DID you think you were going to do?" Danny was looking sideways at Tom as they rode through a vast pasture at the Duke Ranch. Jesper Duke was a man of few words. After brief introductions and what passed for small talk, he offered a good meal and information if they cared to follow him and his men back to his farm. Half an hour later, and he still hadn't spoken to them again.

"How's your head?" Tom asked, totally ignoring Danny's question. She knew he would, since there was no logical explanation for him attempting to fight off a hoard of thieves with only one knife.

Deciding to let it go, she poked gingerly at the small cut in the center of a fading goose egg near her hairline—a parting gift from their stay at FEMA Shelter M3. "She wasn't that tough," Danny joked, and then saw that Tom was still scrutinizing her.

"Really. It hardly hurts. Dad always said I was hardheaded. Guess he was right."

"How do we know these guys aren't going to try and steal all of our stuff, too?" Ethan whispered, moving up in between them. He and Sam had turned back as soon as they'd heard the gunfire, so it was a good thing Jesper and his men showed up when they did.

"It would have already happened if that was his intention," Sam replied, guiding his horse in between Ethan and Danny.

Riding four abroad, Danny appraised all the men to her left and realized what a motley-looking crew they were. The bruises covering Tom and Ethan's faces were still fading, and the cut above Tom's eye was swollen and scabbed over. Danny's fresh wound on her forehead was just as unsightly, and while Sam didn't sport any obvious injuries, his Hispanic complexion wasn't enough to hide the pallor from his illness. He was improving every day and Danny was relieved to see him returning to his old, animated self, but he still looked sickly.

In addition to their rough appearance, they were all dressed in the black garb of the FEMA shelter. Danny could only imagine what they must have looked like to the rancher, and she was curious as to why they'd come to their aid without question.

Jesper Duke chose that moment to glance back at them, and Danny caught his eye. "Mr. Duke," she called out, spurring her horse forward to catch up with the man. "Why did you help us?" Danny gestured to her face first and then tugged at her black T-shirt. "I mean, I'm sure the whole botched black-ops look is enticing, but it's not the friendliest getup."

Jesper chuckled and scratched at his beard. "Most of us here in Graham County have pulled together and done right by each other. However, Nelson and his group chose to go it on their own and have resorted to attacking and taking what they want. He's always been a problem with the law so it wasn't much of a surprise. When we heard that first shot, we were on our way back from a scouting trip. I figured someone was in trouble."

"My father has a tendency to act first and ask questions later. Much later," a man riding to Jesper's right added. He looked to be around Tom's age, in his mid-thirties.

The other five men were riding behind them, and Danny guessed it was as much for safety from Nelson's group as it was to keep a good eye on their group. While Jesper might be a trusting soul, it was clear that his son wasn't.

"We appreciate your intervention," Sam said. "We've had enough setbacks during our travels."

They had come within sight of a large ranch house and Danny's breath caught when she happened to turn to look at it. Though the sprawling estate was impressive, it was the mountains and farmland surrounding it that was extraordinary. Danny was a poor judge of size, but she had to guess hundreds of acres of pasture spread out from it, spotted with clusters of trees and a couple of ponds. Although it wasn't that late in the afternoon, the mountains to the west were so incredibly tall, that the sun was already dipping down behind the ridgeline. It reminded Danny of the Grand Tetons and she could imagine the raw beauty of it in the winter, when it was covered in snow.

"We don't have to go over *those*, do we?" Ethan balked.

Tom reached out and slapped his son on the back. "Not quite, but we do have some mountains to get over before reaching Mercy."

Jesper Duke turned his horse to face them then, forcing the group to stop. Pushing up on the brim of his hat, he eyed Tom closely. "Your friend was right to question my eagerness to invite you out here to the ranch, Thomas. The truth is that I knew your father. Bought some cattle from him, oh...about seven years back."

"I thought your name sounded familiar," Tom answered, offering one of his rare smiles.

Danny watched the exchange with interest. She didn't pretend to know anything about cattle ranching, but figured it wasn't unusual for two large spreads in the same state to be familiar with each other.

"I was sorry to hear of your father's passing," Jesper said, resting his hands on the saddle horn. "You know, our families did business dating back several generations."

It wasn't so much a question, so Tom simply nodded in response.

"In fact, my grandfather's last official cattle drive was through the Old Miner's Pass," Jesper said with a wink.

Tom sat up straight and his smile faded to a look of serious curiosity. "They ran cattle here from our ranch?"

"Yes, sir!" Jesper slapped at his knee, causing Tango to snort and toss his head.

Tom ignored the horse and leaned forward. "How is that possible? I thought that trail put out far north of the interstate."

Chuckling again, Jesper repositioned his hat and turned his horse back. "Join us for supper and I'll explain the mystery," he called over his shoulder, spurring his horse on.

"Why does that matter?" Danny asked, falling in next to Tom. He was still smiling, and she wasn't sure how she felt about it.

"I was planning on using that trail for the last leg of our trip," Tom explained, his voice eager. "It leads directly to my property and will cut about half a day's ride from the journey. Mr. Duke is suggesting that there's another trail near here that connects them."

Danny nodded in understanding. The sooner they got off the roads, the better. And if it also meant shaving even *more* time from the trek, they could be home a day sooner than she thought. Her smile matched Tom's. She'd forgotten how optimism felt.

"Jesper Duke, what have you brought home this time?"

Danny was surprised to see how quickly they had closed in on the house, and saw that a woman had come out to greet them. Though her comment could have been taken as an insult, her tone left no doubt that it was an ongoing joke with her husband. Jesper's son waved to his mom in passing before leading the other five riders away from the front yard and toward a massive barn in the distance.

Jesper dismounted with ease and removed his hat. "Anna, I'd like for you to meet Thomas Miller, of the Miller ranch up in Mercy. This is his son, Ethan, and their two riding companions, Sam and Danny."

Anna Duke stood with her hands on her hips and studied each of them in turn. Her long red hair was arranged in a loose braid, and she wore a blue flannel shirt tucked into blue jeans. She was a tall, sturdy woman and how Danny imagined Tom's mother would look.

Danny didn't know why she suddenly felt a need to impress Anna, but she did her best to sit straight in the saddle, and couldn't stop herself from smoothing down some stray hair.

The older woman smiled then and clapped her hands together. "Jesper, you brought me a woman! Glory be." Shooing at him, she walked straight at Danny. "Now, you get down off that horse and come inside with me while they go put up the horses."

Danny hesitated and again questioned why she was wavering in the face of something positive. Perhaps it was because she'd been stuck in survival mode for so long that she was having a hard time processing things any other way. While the invitation to go inside a nice home for the first time in two weeks was clearly appealing, a large part of her wanted to say with the men, dirty barn and all.

"It's okay," Tom offered. "We'll come find you."

Encouraged, and also appreciative of his understanding, Danny slid from the saddle, landing next to Anna. The rancher threw her arms around her in a huge bear hug, and Danny thought Anna would have lifted her off her feet and swung her around if she'd been able. Large as Anna was, Danny was still bigger.

Laughing, Danny returned the embrace, though she suffered a small bout of anxiety when she heard the horses trotting away. Separating, she was met by a pair of the greenest eyes she'd ever seen. They sparkled with a contagious energy and Danny immediately like the woman.

"I'm Danny Latu," she offered. "It's really great to meet you, Anna. Your husband literally saved our lives when we were attacked."

Anna's smile faded and she took another step back, her hands falling again to her hips. "Nelson?"

"Yeah, that's what Mr. Duke called him."

"Oh, you better call him Jesper," Anna admonished. "Or else that man's superiority complex will get even worse."

Danny laughed at the obvious joke. "Okay. Jesper said it was Nelson and his gang. They ambushed us."

Anna was shaking her head, and already walking back toward the house, expecting Danny to follow. "That man has always been a bad apple. Funny how an event like this brings the boils to the surface."

Danny cringed at the accurate analogy, rushing to keep up with Anna's quick steps. She got the impression the older woman always moved like she had a purpose. "Trust me, we've encountered several different…infections over the past two weeks."

The broad porch wrapped around the whole front of the house and Danny could imagine sitting out on the wooden furniture with a cup of coffee, watching the sun rise over the open view to the east. Anna didn't even pause though, and pulled the double doors open with a flourish. The interior was what Danny would expect of a ranch house: rich wood floors, mahogany trim, large open rooms filled with overstuffed leather furniture, and plenty of windows.

There were oil lamps sitting on several surfaces, as well as a few candles. "I know it may seem like a waste," Anna said, waving at one of the lit candles. "Ever since the…um, event, I can't handle being in the dark. Even the shadows of my home during the day. It's a good thing I make candles, or else I'd have a bit of a problem, now wouldn't I?"

Danny understood then that the brave, strong facade Anna hid behind had some cracks. Everyone's did. "If I had candles, I would keep them lit, too," Danny answered gently.

Anna bobbed her head sharply in response and clapped her hands together again. "Now! When was the last time you used a working toilet or took a bath?"

An hour later, and after several pots of heated water, Danny emerged from Anna Duke's bathroom feeling more rejuvenated than she had since the whole horrible nightmare had begun. The clawfoot tub was better than any spa she'd been to and although she chose to keep her versatile FEMA duty pants, the fresh T-shirt and underclothes Anna gave her were a welcome change.

Wiping at her damp hair with a towel, Danny made her way down the long back hallway and toward the kitchen, where she could hear several voices engaged in a lively conversation. The smell of something cooking was enough to make her mouth water, and the sense of near-normalcy made her eyes well with emotion. She'd forgotten what it was like to be clean and to feel safe.

Rounding the corner, Danny was greeted by Tom, Ethan, and Jesper sitting at a large kitchen table, a map spread out between them. Sam was standing at the counter with Anna, chopping food to add to a pot of something amazing simmering on top of the woodstove.

Tom looked up and his eyes widened when he saw her, taking in her more formfitting shirt and clean hair. Offering a crooked smile, he gestured to the map. "We waited for you," he explained, referring back to her comment about his and Sam's man-time.

Danny grinned. She hated reading maps and was horrible at it. Sitting in the vacant seat next to Tom, she leaning forward eagerly. "So, what's the quickest way home?"

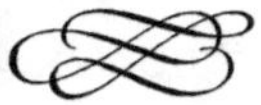

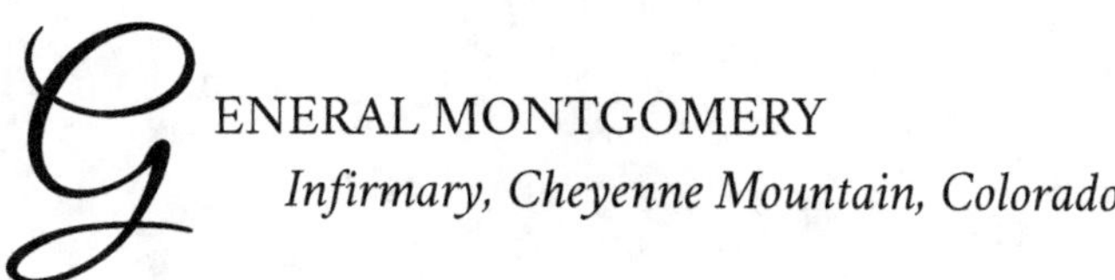

CHAPTER 6

GENERAL MONTGOMERY
Infirmary, Cheyenne Mountain, Colorado

GENERAL MONTGOMERY SIGHED AUDIBLY when he saw Walsh appear at the doorway to his room. "I knew you'd find me eventually, but—" he started to raise his wrist to check the time, out of habit, and stopped with it halfway to his face, sighing again. "You got here a couple of hours faster than I thought you would."

Colonel Walsh scratched at his forehead before pointing at the IV bag hanging by the bed. "You okay?"

A nurse who had just hung the fluids hesitated, looking back and forth between the two men. The general glared at her before barking, "You're dismissed!"

Scurrying from the room, she glanced nervously at Walsh on her way out. He offered an apologetic smile before moving past her and closing the door. "You know there's a fully functioning hospital topside that comes with a much better view."

"This is more than adequate," the general declared, waving a hand. "I'm fine. Just a little dehydrated. And I prefer to stay where there's likely to be more…discretion."

"I found you."

Montgomery laughed halfheartedly. "But you aren't the norm, Colonel Walsh." Pushing himself up further in the bed, he fought a spell of dizziness while leveling the colonel with his steely eyes. By no means would he reveal he was symptomatic, or else he'd never hear the end of it. "I'm assuming there's a reason you're looking for me. Do you have an update on the list?"

"Yes, sir," Walsh confirmed. "I'm handling it personally, like you requested. Out of the sixty-five hundred, I was able to arbitrarily eliminate over four thousand names, based solely on their addresses. There are obvious flaws with this process, of course, but considering the circumstances it's the best we can do."

"Understandable," Montgomery mumbled, eager for the other man to get on with it. He didn't enjoy holding a meeting while lying in a bed. It made him appear weak and not in control. It simply wasn't acceptable. Next time…if there *was* a next time, he'd be sure to visit the infirmary while everyone else was asleep.

"Sir?"

General Montgomery looked up at Walsh with annoyance. "What, Colonel?"

"I asked if you wanted a complete breakdown of the numbers."

"Oh." The general fought another wave of wooziness as he tried to concentrate on the question. "Yes. Yes, of course I want the details."

Colonel Walsh narrowed his eyes and pursed his lips. "Are you sure you're okay? Have you been sleeping?"

Walsh knew full well that he hadn't been sleeping most nights, and Montgomery resented the fact that he pretended otherwise. Insomnia was nothing new for the general. He'd successfully dealt with it before and he would do so again. "Unless there's been a sudden change in status and you now have doctor in front of your name, let's stick to what you know best."

His cheeks flushing, Walsh accepted the reprimand without missing a beat. "It's been difficult to narrow the list down much further," he continued, sitting on the only small plastic chair in the room. "Based on our contacts and the reports coming out of the western states, I created what I'm calling the 'secondary' list. They are assets that I've deemed less likely to still be alive, considering age and location. Such as an eighty-year-old in the middle of Seattle, versus a forty-something in the suburbs of Montana."

Montgomery was nodding. "Good. What does it leave us with?"

"Just over eleven hundred people," Walsh answered. Folding his hands in his lap, he leaned forward, his expression grim. "I issued orders last night. It's going to be slow, and we'll be lucky if we ever have confirmation on even half of those names, but we do have some initial results."

Montgomery raised an eyebrow. "Really?"

Smiling, Walsh was obviously proud to have surprised the general. "Two hard contacts and three soft. A unit near Las Vegas successfully extracted their asset this morning. It's going to take a few days, but they're en route here."

"And the other?" Montgomery asked.

Walsh sat back, his demeanor changing. "Well, sir, there were some complications. We didn't foresee an asset refusing to be saved, which is what happened. He's some sort of high-profile computer programmer in Los Angeles. He was more than content to stay at his mansion in the hills of Hollywood with his family."

He could feel his face reddening. Montgomery had a hard time when his soldiers were unable to think for themselves.

Taking a slow breath, he chose his words carefully. "Colonel Walsh, there seems to be a lack of communication here. These extractions aren't optional. I expect, when an asset is located alive, they *will* be brought in. There are to be no discussions or choices given. Are we clear on this?"

"Yes, sir."

Montgomery always knew when his friend had a problem with orders. However, one of the reasons Walsh had successfully been his assistant for so many years was his ability to keep his opinions to himself and simply say "yes, sir".

"I'm sending Major Campbell and his 1st Force Recon team out for one of the soft contacts. They're already on their way and should arrive on site sometime this afternoon," Walsh continued, correctly anticipating the general's next question. "She's in a hot zone near Albuquerque, New Mexico."

"That's getting awfully close to the red zone for radiation exposure," Montgomery pointed out. "How do you know she's alive?"

"We set up our FEMA command center for New Mexico at the Kirtland AFB in Albuquerque," Walsh explained. "You're right, they've been hit pretty hard with radiation sickness. However, turns out that with the help of the asset, they were able to successfully treat several occupants at the shelter."

"Who is it?" Montgomery's curiosity was piqued. He hadn't spent much time poring over the names and only recognized a couple dozen. He didn't really care why they were deemed important.

"Some astrophysicist," Walsh said, tapping at his thigh. "Apparently she's very knowledgeable about gamma-ray bursts. We're lucky she's still alive." He hesitated.

"What?" Montgomery asked. It was apparent the man had something else to say.

"Conditions there have broken down dramatically over the

past week," Walsh said with enough reservation that Montgomery knew he was being conservative in the estimation. "We've been unable to reach them with sufficient supplies or personnel to make a difference. The base was overrun two days ago and has been under siege ever since."

"Sounds like a perfect mission for 1st Force Recon." The IV drip was about to run dry and the general wanted to end the conversation before the pump alarm brought the nurse back. He briefly considered the irony of his begrudging one of the perks of the EMP-hardened infirmary. "What's the problem?"

Walsh squirmed in the hard chair. "Vice Admiral Baker. He found out Corporal Dillinger was left in charge of FEMA Shelter M3. With the other reports coming in these past two days about the, um…skirmishes breaking out near the other shelters, he's kicked up his opposition."

"Define 'opposition,'" Montgomery said, his voice dangerous.

"He's been having meetings," Walsh admitted, staring down at his hands. "With Major O'Shane and a few of the advisors. He's also been in contact with some of the remaining civilian state government. Especially those who have been opposed to the martial law declaration and ensuing federal takeover."

"To what end?" Montgomery pushed. "He can talk to whomever he wants. He doesn't have the power or influence to do anything about it."

"He's made comments that lead me to believe he's going to use the 1st Force Recon missions as examples of military attacks against civilians," Walsh said, finally getting to the heart of the matter.

The pump started beeping. The general reached out and yanked the cord from the wall with enough force to send the machine crashing to the ground. As the working end of the IV ripped from his arm, Montgomery slapped his other hand over the site without even looking. Blood oozed from between his fingers as he stared at Walsh, nostrils flaring.

"I want a complete report on the vice admiral's activities," he growled.

The door opened and a frightened nurse stuck her head in.

"I'm fine!"

The door closed.

"I want to know who he's met with, who he's talking to, and what's being said," the general continued.

Walsh stood then, and looked uncertain as to whether he should comment on the blood that was spreading out on the blanket under the general's arm. Wisely choosing to let it go, he instead moved toward the door. "Yes, sir."

"Colonel?"

Walsh stopped with his hand on the door and looked back.

"Where is the admiral residing now?"

"He's still on the top floor of building three," Walsh answered, looking somewhat confused.

"Has he been outside the mountain since the flashpoint?" Montgomery asked, thoughtful.

Walsh shook his head.

Montgomery wrapped his fingers more tightly around his forearm, effectively cutting off the flow of blood. "Perhaps it's time for the good admiral to get some fresh air."

CHAPTER 7

$\mathcal{J}$AMES
> *Master Sergeant, US Marines, 1ˢᵗ Force Recon-*
> *naissance*
> *Albuquerque, New Mexico*

JAMES DIDN'T LIKE IT, but there was no other way. Both the INFIL and EXFIL were going to be messy. The Kirtland Air Force Base was located at the southern end of Albuquerque, and the main buildings were literally surrounded by a heavily populated area. With over half a million residing in the city, it was a large metropolis with no clear path in or out. The only support 1ˢᵗ Force Recon had was the helicopter, and with no other means of transportation, they were forced to go with a direct insert.

Since being subtle was off the board, the obvious infiltration point was the international airport adjacent to the base. It also happened to be close to the military medical center, where Dr. Pamela Watson was last reported to be holed up.

"I thought this chick was an astronomer or something," Jay

shouted over the hum of the Huey. "What's she doing acting like a doctor?"

James stared at his friend long enough to convey his displeasure with the question. Gunnery Sergeant Jay Terrill was his second and knew they were supposed to keep the details of the assets to a minimum. "It's not our job to ask questions, Terrill."

The intel from the limited communication with Cheyenne Mountain was sparse. Most of it was from previous exchanges regarding FEMA Shelter NM1, which was originally erected in the fields at the southern end of the Kirtland Air Force base. Like so many other failed attempts in other states, the personnel had underestimated the threat from the civilian population and was overrun in a matter of days. Already suffering from varying degrees of radiation sickness, the survivors surrendered the shelter and fell back to the clinic and a couple of attached, defendable buildings.

Dr. Pamela Watson had become involved sometime soon after the flashpoint, apparently going to the military base in an attempt to pass on useful information regarding the gamma-ray burst. That was the only reason her name was flagged, and the unconfirmed location deemed a soft contact. The base had gone silent for more than two days.

As the Huey moved within a few klicks of their insertion point, James turned to address his men. "I know we're not used to operating without a TOC, but we just stick with the plan. Lance and Flores, you keep your heads on a swivel and protect Helo 1 at all costs. She's our only ride out."

Though the 1st Force Reconnaissance unit was an elite group of highly trained Marines, they usually had plenty of support, including a Tactical Operations Center. As it was, they were lucky to have one helicopter, and even more fortunate to have comms. The TASC headsets were a parting gift from Corporal Walsh before they'd left the mountain. James didn't know how or why the tactical radios had been stored at Cheyenne, and he didn't care. All that mattered was that with the ability to communicate with each other on the ground, they at least stood a better chance of pulling off a successful operation.

"We treat it like any other snatch-and-grab," Sergeant Lee added as he secured his headgear and comms.

James watched as his team did their weapons and gear checks, then turned his attention back to the darkening landscape. It was spotted with fires and what looked like clusters of people scattered throughout the city. If a night op had been feasible, they would have done it, but it was nearly impossible to navigate over long distances without visual flight. No satellites meant no GPS, whether their instruments had power or not.

"There," James directed, pointing to the airstrip. A good portion of the airport was burned, but the buildings to the east were intact. Those were the target. "Get us as close as possible."

The downside to having the medical center next to an airport was that there was no need for them to have a landing pad on their roof, as some other hospitals did. And while they were only a parking lot away, it was an open span where they would all be vulnerable to anyone with a gun. People would already be responding to the incredible and sudden appearance of the helicopter so the clock was ticking.

As the Huey touched down, James launched himself out of the opening and hit the ground moving forward in a crouching run. He knew without looking back that the three other soldiers were behind him.

They hadn't gone more than a hundred yards when four military personnel came running toward them, likely having the same reaction to the helicopter as everyone else nearby. James slowed but didn't stop, and raised his M4 to the ready. "Identify yourselves!"

The three men and one woman were in filthy fatigues, and

only two of them were armed. "Airman Johnson!" the nearest man shouted, raising his empty hands. "We're from the Kirtland base. Who are you, special ops? Thank God you're here."

"Where's the rest?" the woman said, stopping and looking over at the helicopter in a daze. "There's more of you, right?" Her eyes widened as she realized the four soldiers in front of her were the sum of the assumed rescue team.

"Master Sergeant Campbell, 1st Force Reconnaissance," James barked, not lowering his weapon. "I'm looking for Dr. Pamela Watson."

"What do you want with Pamela?" the first man asked, looking around nervously. "She's inside," he rushed to add, motioning back over his shoulder and toward the clinic. "But we can't stay out here, man. It's not safe."

"Two tangos on my left," Jay shouted. "Moving fast."

James pivoted, bringing his Carbine around and quickly lining it up with two men who were skirting around some vehicles a couple hundred feet away. "Alpha Three, give me some suppression fire."

Sergeant Lee complied with a short burst of automatic fire that sent chunks of cement flying near the advancing men's feet. As expected, they dove for cover and James felt fairly certain that the show of fire power would be enough to buy them a few extra minutes.

"Dr. Watson," James repeated, turning back to the wary soldiers. "I need you to take us to her."

"This way," Airman Johnson called as he ran back the way they'd come.

"Alpha One to Helo One," James spoke into his headset.

"Go for Helo One."

"We have confirmation on the HVT and are moving in for retrieval." James knew the likelihood of anyone else having the ability to listen in on their conversation was remote, but it was still protocol. And Dr. Pamela Watson was most definitely a Highly Valued Target.

"Helo One copies."

"Alpha Five to Alpha One."

"Go for Alpha One." James tried to keep the irritation out of his voice. He didn't want to stand around and talk and Flores always had a big mouth.

"We've got at least a dozen tangos inbound from the FEMA shelter location."

James passed up the slower airman and headed for the main entrance of the hospital. They'd have to make it fast. Grunting with dissatisfaction, he keyed up his radio. "Do what you can without any casualties, Alpha Five. Get ready for EXFIL."

The parking lot was three-quarters full of useless vehicles, some of them burned, as well as several bodies in various stages of decomposition. That they were left to rot spoke of the hopeless situation the people there were facing.

Two more armed soldiers met them at the doors, looking both shocked and hopeful. Airman Johnson waved them off and they looked too weak to put up any resistance.

"She's upstairs," the female soldier offered, leading the way toward a stairwell.

She bent to pick up the candle stub left near the door, but Jay stopped her. "We've got it," he offered, snapping on a flashlight.

It was remarkable, the effect a simple light had on the group. A collective gasp was followed by silence, and that was when James was hit by the stench as he opened the door to the stairs. Taking a step back, he raised a hand to his face and resisted the urge to gag.

"What is *that*?" Sergeant Lucas O'Grady gasped.

They had all experienced the smell of death, the worst of it at the Mount Weather facility. But the smell wafting over them was like nothing James had ever encountered. A mix of decay, feces, urine, and a putridness he couldn't and didn't want to identify.

"Welcome to hell," Airman Johnson said, his voice hollow. "Death by radiation is a slow, messy process. The lucky ones died the first week. The not so lucky? Well, they're still suffering in their own bloody soup of waste."

"Shut up!" the woman shouted, pushing the man forward and onto the first of the metal steps. "It's the worst in here," she explained, looking back at James as he forced himself to follow, wishing he'd thought to bring their masks. "We didn't have anywhere else to put the bodies…hundreds of them. So, they're stacked in the basement, along with all the garbage and waste. It's not that bad, unless you open a door."

James's eyes burned from ammonia as they climbed the stairs and he was relieved when they exited on the third floor, instead of the sixth. They were greeted by a group of people gathered in some sort of lounge area next to the stairwell. James figured it was originally a waiting room. While it was impossible for him to have a picture of the doctor, he knew that she was a fifty-two-year-old African American woman, so could see immediately that she wasn't part of the crowd.

"Dr. Pamela Watson!" James shouted. His loud, booming voice echoed off the cement walls and several of the people cringed away from him. While a couple were in fatigues, the rest were wearing regular clothes, all of them covered in filth. Dim, flickering light provided from several candles lit the room, and it was enough to reveal the sorry state the survivors were in.

"What's happened?" a woman called out as she ran down a connecting hallway. "I thought I heard gunshots after the helicopter landed." She froze when she saw James and the rest of the unit.

"Dr. Pamela Watson?" Lowering his rifle, James did his best to look less intimidating.

Dr. Watson squinted at him, taking in his uniform and equipment. "You have working radios and a helicopter. I'll be whoever you want me to be." When he only glared at her in response, she grinned. "You bet I'm Dr. Watson! It's about time help got here. What's your plan? We've got a hundred and eighteen left alive."

James could see Jay shifting uneasily from foot to foot, and he could feel time slipping by. He didn't like to stand still while on an op and they'd already been inside the building for too long.

"Helo One to Alpha One."

"Go for Alpha One," James answered, turning away from the doctor.

"We're getting too hot for extraction. Suppression is no longer working. We'll need to use lethal force."

"That's a hard copy," James barked, thinking through the options, which weren't many. "Move to secondary EXFIL."

"Copy that. Moving to secondary extraction point. Five mikes."

James spun back to face Dr. Watson before the transmission had even finished. "I'm here to retrieve you, Doctor. We can discuss the others on the way out."

"Nanna!" a young girl of around five years old broke off from the group in the waiting room and ran to Doctor Watson, wrapping her small arms around her grandmother's legs. "Are we going home? Can we get some water? I'm still thirsty."

Pamela reached down and placed a hand on top of the girl's curly hair while staring at James, her dark eyes welling with tears. She began to shake her head and then slowly pointed a finger at him. "No. I'm not going anywhere until all of us have a ride out of this nightmare."

James was acutely aware of the two armed soldiers who had followed them upstairs, as well as the growing crowd in the waiting room. More survivors, in various degrees of illness and despair, were slowly making their way towards the commotion from three different darkened hallways. While he trusted his own men and knew they would be restrained in their reactions, their orders were clear and failure wasn't an option.

Looking back down at the little girl, James made a decision he knew he'd have to live with for the rest of his life. Stepping forward he leaned in close and spoke inches away from the doctor's face. "We need to have a private conversation."

A flash of fear crossed her face and her fingers curled into her granddaughter's hair.

"She can come," James offered before gesturing towards what looked like an office behind a reception area.

Dr. Watson led the way, and James closed the door behind them, raising his other hand at the same time she started to talk. "Let me be clear. You have two choices. You can either cooperate, and leave with us under the guise that you're helping us coordinate a rescue, and bring your granddaughter. Otherwise, I'll throw you over my shoulder and you'll still leave. Alone."

"But I—"

"You'll make your decision by the time I open this door. We're leaving now. Is there a way to the roof?" Dr. Watson nodded, and James pushed at the door.

Stepping back out into the room, he smiled at the other people. "Dr. Watson has agreed to help us organize your rescue. Airman!" Airman Johnson jerked to attention. "I need you to get ready. Separate those who can and can't walk. I want these people ready to move by the time I get back. Understood?"

Not waiting for an answer, James motioned to Jay and then glanced at the doctor. She was holding tightly to her granddaughter's hand and stoically waving to the people who only moments before she thought she'd never leave. It was cruel, but there was no other way. The Huey could only hold a few more passengers and the clinic was about to be overrun.

They re-entered the stairwell and headed for the roof. Two minutes later they burst onto the top of the six-story building, where Helo One was waiting, hovering, a SPIE rope deployed below it. Already forming a plan on how to raise both the doctor and young girl to safety, James noticed movement below them in the parking lot.

The group advancing from what remained of the FEMA shelter had reached the clinic. Distracted by the recon team and outnumbered, the guards at the doors were easily overtaken. They were shooting randomly into the growing mob, but James knew it wouldn't make a difference.

Jay easily lifted the little girl while James reached for Dr. Watson, but she grabbed ahold of him first as her legs buckled. Sobbing, her eyes burned with a fury and pain he'd never seen before. "You've killed them all," she spat.

James grit his teeth and wrapped her up in his massive arms. "They were already dead."

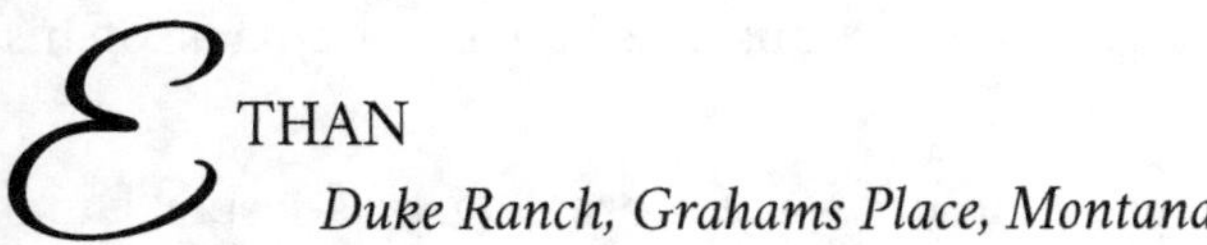

CHAPTER 8

ETHAN

Duke Ranch, Grahams Place, Montana

THE FIRE SNAPPED as sap exploded and sent a cascade of sparks up into the sky. Ethan stared into it, finding it both mesmerizing and relaxing. He'd spent hours that way when he'd been held captive by Decker and Billy. It was the only time with them when he wasn't scared.

"Hey."

Ethan jumped, and then smiled up at Sam as the older man eased himself down to the ground next to him. It might have been wishful thinking, but Ethan thought Sam looked better than he had just that morning. Cutting their travel for the day in half and having a good meal probably had a lot to do with it.

"Mind if I join you?" Sam leaned back against the log Ethan was using and then reached out to pet Grace, who was laying curled up at Ethan's feet and halfway across his lap.

Ethan shrugged. "Sure, Sam. I'm just getting warmed up before bed. Looks like it might be a wet night."

Sam looked up at the sky that had turned dark and ominous soon after dinner. Ethan was glad the northern lights were finally blocked from view, but the idea of a storm wasn't too appealing. While they would be sleeping in a dry bunkhouse that night, it could still mean a messy ride the next day.

An odd flash of orange light briefly lit the mountains to their southwest, and the air remained eerily silent and heavy. Ethan turned to get a better look at where the storm was building, but it was too dark to really make out much. Another burst of color caused the bottom of the clouds to glow, this time with more of a whitish-blue tinge. He'd seen plenty of storms, growing up in Montana, and this one was making the hair on the back of his neck rise.

"It appears that we're in for some more changes," Jesper Duke said from across the fire. He sat on a large stump, one booted ankle crossed over the other. Danny and his dad sat next to Jesper, and Anna moved forward with a large piece of wood to toss on the fire, nodding at her husband in agreement.

It was obvious to Ethan that there were a lot of nights spent talking around the fire. It was positioned centrally between the main house, barn, and bunk house. Jesper's son, as well as the five farmhands who came to their rescue earlier that day, were spread around the campfire talking animatedly amongst themselves.

"There's a good chance the weather is going to get worse," Sam offered, drawing everyone's attention. He shifted slightly as he gathered his thoughts and Ethan absently rubbed at Grace's ears while he listened. "The gamma-ray burst must have destroyed a large percentage of the ozone layer, as well as disrupted the chemical compounds in the upper atmosphere. This could have a cascading effect on the weather systems, including the jet stream."

"Are we talking Tornado Alley moving over a couple of states, or hurricanes in the desert sort of stuff?" Anna Jesper asked, sounding more annoyed than scared.

Sam tossed a stick at the fire and made a tsking noise. "Impossible to say, really, but I'd think at the minimum, there's a potential for storms larger than anything experienced in recent history."

"And the temperature?" One of the cowhands asked, pulling his jacket closed. "It shouldn't be this cold at night. Not in June."

"The temperature, weather, plant die-off, and maybe even a form of acid rain," Sam confirmed. "The fallout could go on for years."

"Plant die-off," Jesper echoed. He sounded troubled but Ethan was having a hard time reading the older man's expression in the firelight. "We've been noticing the pines in the higher elevations have been dropping their needles early, and the tops are turning brown."

"Is that from the gamma radiation?" Jesper's son asked.

"No." Ethan was surprised to hear his dad answer the question. "It's from the ultraviolet radiation."

"Right, Tom," Sam confirmed. "The ozone acts as a buffer for several different elements, including the sun's radiation."

"Then why in the world is it getting *colder*?" another one of the hands pressed.

"Higher UV doesn't necessarily mean more heat," Sam tried to explain. "And in addition to the ozone layer damage, the chemical changes are contributing to the temperature fluctuations. Look, I'm not going to try and pretend like I have all of the answers, because I don't. It's all speculation on my part."

Another eerie strobe of orange and then blue punctuated his words, and Ethan wished they'd change the subject. It would be great if they could pretend that things were normal. Just for a little while.

Anna stood back up then and slapped at her thighs. "Come on, Danny."

Danny looked surprised, and didn't move from where she was on the stump, next to Tom. "Where are we going?"

Anna waved a hand in the general direction of the bunkhouse. "While I'm sure these men find the bunkhouse to be more than adequate, it's no place for a lady. My daughter is gone with a hunting party so you're more than welcome to her room."

Ethan was confused by Danny's reaction, as she sat there looking back and forth between their host, Sam, and Tom. If he'd been the one offered a private room with a big bed, he would have already been halfway across the yard.

The older woman, on the other hand, took it all in stride. "Don't worry about your friends, we'll be seeing them bright and early. Come on," she took Danny by the hand and pulled her to her feet. "The invitation also includes a cup of tea and a good, womanly conversation."

Danny finally smiled and laughed lightly. "Okay, Anna. How can I pass that up?" Breaking away from the other woman, Danny walked over and knelt down in front of Sam. "You doing all right?" When he nodded, she gave Sam a quick hug. "Be sure to take your last dose of antibiotics before you go to bed."

Sam gave her a mock salute in response, and she batted his hand away playfully. "Be sure he takes it." She added to Ethan while reaching out to give his arm a squeeze. He understood then why she was hesitant to go. They'd relied upon each other so much over the past ten days that it didn't feel right when they were separated. It was the worst part about being at the FEMA camp.

Ethan watched as Danny waved goodnight to Jesper and then hesitated in front of his dad. He wouldn't have thought anything of it, except for the way Tom looked at her. He started to lift his arms, but then seemed to catch himself and hesitated when

Danny took a step back. His smile wavered as she continued past him to follow Anna.

Closing his eyes, Ethan moaned and leaned his head back against the log.

"What is it?" Sam asked.

Turning his head, Ethan rolled his eyes at Sam. "I don't know if I'll ever understand women."

Sam laughed and elbowed Ethan lightly in the ribs. "That is a pipedream of every man who's ever lived. Give it up now and save yourself a whole lot of grief."

Watching Danny walk away, Ethan's smile faded. He liked her. She was like an older sister or aunt, and he didn't want anything to interfere with the easy friendship they'd developed. His dad had a bad track record when it came to relationships and Ethan didn't want him to do anything that would keep Danny away once they reached Mercy. It would have been better if she'd kept despising Tom. Ethan wasn't even sure when or why that had changed.

Danny paused then and turned back, whistling once for Grace. The retriever's head snapped up and she leapt to her feet when she saw Danny. Grace offered a small whine as she licked Ethan's hand and he patted the back of her neck. "Go on," he said gently. "I understand."

As the dog trotted after Danny, the unease Ethan had been feeling intensified. Once they got home, if Danny went her own way that meant he wouldn't see Grace either...or Sam. Looking again at the older man, Ethan felt a surge of desperation. Since the flashpoint, he'd had to come to terms with the likelihood that he'd never see his mom again, or his home, or friends. His life before was gone. Now, Sam and Danny were an important part of his world and he wasn't sure what he would do if they disappeared from it. He looked back in time to see Grace's tail disappear inside the house and he nearly choked on a sob that threatened to tear loose.

"Sam?" Ethan stammered as another blue bolt of lightning lit the sky. "What's going to happen when we get to Mercy?"

Sam looked nonplussed. "You'll be reunited with your grandmother, and Danny with her dad. What else would happen, Ethan?"

Ethan huffed with frustration and repositioned himself so he was facing Sam. "No, I mean what are we all going to *do*? Where are you going to stay, Sam? Is Danny gonna go back to Helena once she checks on her dad? I might never see Grace again. You might leave—"

"Hey—" Sam interrupted, putting a hand on his shoulder at the same time. "I'm not going to lie and pretend I know how this is all going to play out. But the one thing I'm sure about is that I'm going to always be your friend. We're family now, Ethan, and we're in this together. Through all of it, and that doesn't end just because we get to Mercy. Besides, your dad said there's an extra room at the ranch and I've always wanted to be a cowboy."

Relieved, Ethan smiled back at his friend and then focused again on the fire, afraid that he was going to get emotional. Through the flames, he saw his dad watching him, a look of concern on his hardened face. The sky strobed orange and then blue, casting their group into a melee of bizarre shadows and momentarily changing his father into an unrecognizable form.

Blinking rapidly, Ethan pushed at the ground with his feet, forcing his back painfully into the log behind him as he was plunged into a memory of the horrific night in Pocatello. As the light faded, so did the vision, leaving Ethan gasping for air. It was a vivid reminder that nothing was what it seemed anymore. Even in Mercy, he would never truly be home again.

CHAPTER 9

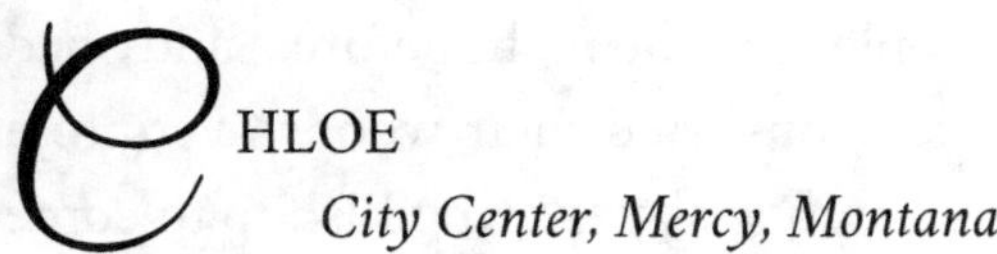

CHLOE

City Center, Mercy, Montana

CHLOE HAD NEVER LIKED CROWDS. She found it hard enough to pretend to be interested in regular conversations, and when you stuck a bunch of people together in the same space, all talking at once, it was enough to make her want to scream.

Sitting at the picnic table across from Sandy and Bishop, the hardest part for Chloe wasn't so much the noise as it was the fact that everyone was trying so hard to act like everything was okay. Except it wasn't. It never would be.

"Aren't you going to finish your steak?" Trevor asked while lightly elbowing Chloe in the ribs.

Snatching the plate away, she slid it out of his reach. "Don't you even *think* about it. I actually worked for this meal and I want to take my time enjoying it."

Trevor's face scrunched up as he grasped the not-so-subtle criticism. "Hey, I worked all day at the clinic, and then I spent the past four hours delivering water and meals to people who couldn't come to the barbeque."

"Never mind Miss Killjoy," Crissy said flippantly. "She's been grouchy all day."

As was often the case, Chloe fought to keep from answering Crissy with an even snarkier remark. As much as the younger girl drove her crazy at times, she was the best friend Chloe ever had and was one of the few people in her life who could keep her in check. Besides, Crissy was right. She'd been looking for a fight all afternoon.

"I wanted to thank you personally, Sandy."

Chloe was saved from herself by Patty's well-timed interruption. The mayor was standing at the end of the picnic table, holding an honest-to-God apple pie. The night before, Sandy had been talking about how Caleb converted their woodstove into a working oven and stovetop. Sandy was pestering Bishop to come up with something similar for the ranch, and looking at the pie, Chloe decided to start working on her own design.

"I used your favorite apples," Patty continued when nobody spoke. Setting the pie on the table, she looked pointedly at Sandy. "That steer is more than just a meal for the whole town, it's a symbol of hope. A sign that together, we're going to get through this."

Chloe had been busy helping prepare the last of the food earlier, so she missed the speech the mayor gave to the people gathered in the city center. She had a feeling those two lines were straight from it, making them feel somewhat hollow.

"Thanks, Patty," Sandy answered with a smile. "We all want the same thing. Let's just work together to make sure we do it all the right way."

Patty glanced over her shoulder and then looked nervously at the nearest tables. Without saying anything further, she turned back to Sandy with a dejected expression and gave a small nod before moving on.

To be fair, Chloe didn't envy Mayor Patty's situation. There really wasn't any way to win, and no matter what she did, there would be some people who disagreed with her methods. From the time Chloe had spent with her, she knew Patty was kind and was honestly doing her best under the circumstances.

The circumstances.

Chloe grunted at the thought while stabbing a chunk of meat. Placing the morsel in her mouth, she thought about what Patty said. *Was* it a symbol of hope? Had their lives been so thoroughly stripped away in two weeks that it all came down to a dead cow giving them inspiration?

Chloe chewed slowly, mulling over the meaning of that. She'd been afraid she wouldn't even be able to stomach the meat, after helping lead the steer to the spot near the creek where he was met by a bullet to the head. She had then watched, with a sort of morbid curiosity, as a group of men and women butchered it right there, stripping away the layers and dismembering it.

Like their lives.

Closing her eyes, Chloe sighed and dug deep to find a remnant of joy to grasp onto. While she'd willingly thrown herself into the busy work of survival, the distraction was wearing off. She missed her parents. She missed her room, with its obnoxious purple glitter rug and pictures of the universe taped to the walls. She missed her early morning jogs. Chloe missed her *life.*

Several people laughed at an unheard comment at the next table over, causing Chloe to open her eyes and take in the reality of where she was: the city center in Mercy, Montana. Their second weekly town barbeque, complete with a stage for enter-tainment, which consisted of a guitar-wielding cowboy singing ballads, a row of smoking BBQs, and enough picnic tables to seat half of the town's population.

The rest that could attend had to find random seating that spilled out onto Main Street. She half expected to see a clown emerge with a bundle of balloons, but that would just be weird.

The prep time for the meat had taken longer than expected, so the festivities had gotten off to a late start. Jerry-rigged oil lamps hung from hooks on the steel lamp poles, hooks that Chloe suspected were normally used for hanging flower baskets. They were surprisingly efficient and afforded a decent amount of soft light in both the picnic area as well as on Main Street.

When combined with the old-fashioned western storefronts that adorned most of the buildings on Main Street, it was as if they'd been transported back through time. Horses were tied to the original hitching posts in front of City Hall and the post office. The wagon was constantly rattling up and down the roads, hauling either water or food, or sometimes both. With the water station at the south end of town and the farmer's market at the other, the borders of Mercy were smaller than ever. People waved at each other as they passed on the street and they all had the same, makeup-less, raw uninhibited look to them.

They were moving on. That was what bothered Chloe. No matter how much sense it did or didn't make, she was furious that while the rest of the world fell to pieces, the people of Mercy were simply…*living*.

"Sandy told me you're going to start jogging the Miner trail," Bishop said, interrupting her dark thoughts.

Chloe blinked a couple of times at Bishop, her eyes narrowing. Her initial reaction was irritation that the two of them had been talking about her, and that only caused her anxiety to grow. She could feel herself slipping back into the angry, sometimes violent girl who had landed her in the Trek Thru Trouble club, and she was determined to overcome it.

Her problem was that she wasn't sure how. Actually, that was the whole reason behind the jogging. At home, when Chloe was feeling overwhelmed and her emotions were unchecked, she ran. The physical exercise helped to ground her and she currently needed a whole lot of grounding.

Forcing a smile, she swallowed a bit of mashed potatoes. "Yeah, Sandy said it goes for over a hundred miles, so I figure I won't run out of trail."

Bishop grinned at her joke and then began to cut up the apple pie. "When do you plan on going? Maybe I or Crissy could join you. Being out there alone might not be the best thing right now."

Her smile fading, Chloe lost her tenuous hold on restraint. "Being alone is the whole point, Bishop. I don't need a babysitter. Do you know if Caleb managed to get a hold of anyone in Washington State yet about a survivor list?" she asked, pointedly changing the subject.

"I haven't had much time to sit at the radio with him." Bishop said, shaking his head. Sliding a piece of pie onto Chloe's plate without asking, he then stared at her with his intense blue eyes. "We'll get word to your parents. If we can't find them, I'll take you home next year myself. I promise."

Chloe knew he meant it. Her view of the apple pie blurring, she didn't trust herself to say much. "Okay," she murmured, knowing he would understand and not push for something more.

A new chorus of exclamations and loud chatter arose near the entrance to the courtyard. Chloe strained to see what the commotion was about, half-expecting the clown, after all. Instead, she saw a middle-aged, handsome stranger. He was led by Patty, and Father White was trailing behind him, not looking too pleased. Chloe guessed he was just released from quarantine. She'd heard very little about him, except that he saved one of the

Pony Express riders, and traveled nearly five-hundred miles to keep a promise to a dying man.

"That's the new priest who made it here all the way from Wyoming," Sandy said, her excitement obvious. "He came a different way than Tom and Ethan would," she added, "but if he was able to get here on a bike, then I have no doubt my son will make it."

Chloe didn't point out the fact that the other man traveling with the priest had been killed along the way. It was still hard to comprehend the sort of violence and destruction happening outside their valley, but as more reports from riders and visitors correlated with what Caleb got from the radio, there was no denying it.

"I certainly hope Tom gets here soon. Maybe he can talk some sense into Patty and shed some light on what's really going on with our government," Gary said. The councilman sat down at the table on the other side of Bishop, directly across from Chloe.

She noticed the man's graying hair was still well groomed and that he was clean shaved. Most of the men were allowing their beards to grow out, since they were forced to otherwise use regular razors. It was an aspect of being without power that Chloe had never considered until she'd noticed Bishop's stubble was coming in gray and she'd teased him about it. Clean underwear was another. She had always thought doing laundry the old-fashioned way would be hard because of having to hang it up to dry. Turned out that was the unexpectedly pleasant part, because she loved the way her clothes smelled after drying in a fresh breeze. However, hauling water, boiling it, and then washing the laundry by hand really, really sucked.

She wasn't sure why the observation of Gary the councilman troubled her. Perhaps it was also the tie he wore with the blue dress shirt, and the strong cologne that was burning Chloe's nose. It felt…disrespectful. Like his proper appearance was a mockery of their current existence.

Sandy sighed heavily and leaned forward so she could see around Bishop. "Politics, Gary? We're really going to talk about politics right now?"

Gary's countenance shifted and his lip twitched. "Certainly, you of all people must see what's happening."

"No, I'm afraid I don't," Sandy said, her back stiffening.

Gesturing to the steak left on Chloe's plate, Gary wrinkled his nose at it. "You know this is only the beginning. Tell me, were you given a choice? Or did Patty and one of her supporters tell you it was time to, um…*donate* your stock? The question you need to ask yourself is if that conversation would have played out any differently had Tom been there."

Sandy bristled, but she didn't try and deny it.

"Anyway," Gary said, waving a hand dismissively while standing slowly. "None of it might be necessary if Patty hadn't unilaterally decided to cut us off from our own government."

Bishop frowned at the councilman. "What do you mean by that?"

Bishop's voice was harsh and it had the desired effect on Gary, as he flinched and took a small step back. "You two are such good friends with the good mayor, you should ask her yourselves."

Chloe watched Gary scurry away, and she had a strong feeling he was very much the weasel he appeared to be. However, he'd successfully planted seeds of doubt. She could see it plainly on everyone's faces, including her own. A Fourth-of-July-themed balloon drifted across the grass and Chloe watched as it passed in front of where Patty and the new priest stood, laughing with Sheriff Waters.

Was Mercy not the oasis it seemed to be?

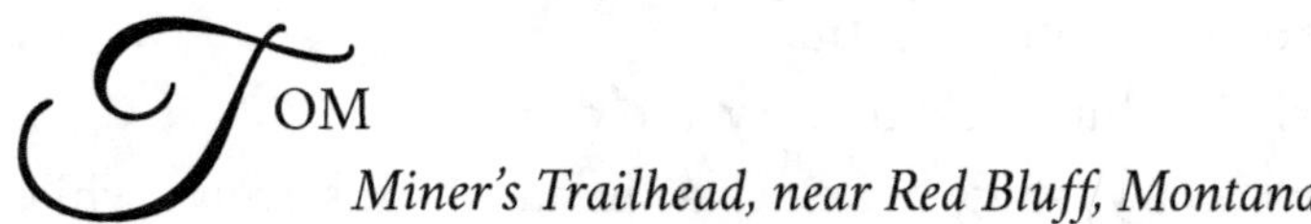

CHAPTER 10

T OM

Miner's Trailhead, near Red Bluff, Montana

TOM HAD to admit to some relief when Jesper Duke finally raised a hand, signaling for the group to stop. They'd been riding hard for the past two hours, since before sunrise. Tom knew that if he was getting sore, Danny and Sam must be miserable.

Ethan, on the other hand, was apparently as resilient as Tango. The two galloped past them after they had stopped and the teen fought momentarily to turn the gelding around. "Are we at the trail already?" he gasped, his breath showing in the cool morning air.

Jesper dismounted while chuckling at Ethan's enthusiasm. "Close enough, son. Before I see you off, I want to show your father something." Looking at Tom, he handed his reins over to his son before gesturing up the road. "On foot from here so we don't make too much noise. Just a mile or so."

Curious, Tom followed suit and jumped down next to the

older man, his legs protesting when they hit the ground. "What is it I need to see?"

"Road block," Jesper explained, setting his gloved hands on his hips. "Old man Patterson lives near here and said it showed up… oh, I figure about four days ago now. Armed men with an attitude."

Tom rubbed at this head, careful not to unsettle the scab above his eye. "Sounds similar to what they've got at the FEMA shelter we came from."

Jesper grunted. "That's what I was thinking, but I was hoping you'd take a look before heading out. After hearing your story, I don't know what would be worse, militia, road bandits, or our own government."

Danny slid off her mare and massaged the backs of her thighs with a pained expression. "I'd like to go."

"Suit yourself," Jesper shrugged, already walking. "We'll make it fast. I know you'd like to get underway before that storm hits about as much as I'd like to make it back home."

Tom squinted up at the ominous clouds that had continued to build for over twelve hours. Just as Sam had predicted, it was like nothing they'd ever seen before. The front wall of the storm appeared to be growing thicker and taller, instead of moving forward, and the resulting wedge reminded him of a massive wave about to crest. It very well could be an accurate analogy, and Jesper was absolutely right. He really didn't want them to be stuck riding in it, especially not on a mountain trail he wasn't familiar with.

Danny was already following Jesper, but she paused when she realized Sam and Ethan weren't with them. Raising her eyebrows, she looked up at Sam, who was very slowly climbing down from his horse. "You coming?"

Moaning when his feet made contact with the dirt on the side of the road, Sam stood motionless with a hand pressed into the small of his back. "You know, I think I'm going to pass and spend this time sitting my butt on the ground once I can move it again."

Danny laughed, and Tom found himself staring at her. She really was quite attractive when she smiled. "Okay, Sam," she said lightly. "You sit here and nurse your backside."

"I'll stay with him," Ethan offered. He was still on Tango and gave a sideways glance to the three other men that had ridden out with them from the ranch. Tom realized in that moment that Ethan was being protective. Even if it was unfounded, it was still a rather mature gesture and made Tom look at his son in a different way.

Grace began licking at Sam's face as soon as he lowered himself enough, and he lovingly pushed her back. Draping an arm around the dog's shoulders, he waved Tom and Danny off. "Go on. I'll last longer if I get a break now."

Tom answered with a simple bob of his head and then he jogged to catch up to Jesper, who was already a good distance up the road. While Sam improved a little each day, he was probably right to take it easy. Based on how Danny fretted over him, Tom guessed Sam was still susceptible to a lung infection. They were so close to home, and it wasn't worth taking any extra risks. Looking again at the tempest looming over them, he wondered if they should have taken Jesper and Anna up on their offer to stay another day.

They had all discussed it, and in the end, both Danny and Sam agreed with Tom. Since they had no idea if they'd get caught in the storm, or how long it would last if they did, it wasn't worth the delay. Tom and Ethan had faced even more setbacks than Danny and Sam, and they were all eager to reach Mercy.

"I hope you'll consider what I told you last night," Tom said as he moved up alongside Jesper. "Corporal Dillinger is a dangerous man. He's only eighty miles or so away from your ranch, and I wouldn't be surprised if his men showed up there."

"That land has been in my family for more than a hundred and fifty years," Jesper said, his voice gruff and resolute.

"If Dillinger decides he wants your cattle, he isn't going to take no for an answer," Danny added, having joined them in time to hear the conversation.

Jesper shook his head, his face cross. "The Dukes have given their lives for the freedom of this country for three generations. Freedom I'm not about to so easily surrender for my son and grandkids."

"If his men *do* come," Tom urged. "Try to negotiate with them. They might listen to reason, but not defiance."

Jesper scratched thoughtfully at the scruff on his jaw as they continued to walk. The morning fog hadn't yet burned all the way off of the thick woods lining the road, making it feel as if they were walking through a misty, magical land full of dragons. When he stopped suddenly and put a hand up, Tom half-expected something surreal to come charging out of the trees.

"Is that a helicopter?" Danny asked, her eyes widening in fear.

Tom heard it then, too. The low *whoop whoop* of the blades cutting through the air. He looked to the sky but all he could see were clouds.

"This way," Jesper ordered, and led them into the trees to the right side of the road. "The barricade is right around this next bend."

Sure enough, they'd hardly trekked more than fifty feet through the dense underbrush before Tom could hear a distinct conversation between three men in the distance. They were arguing about what was the best MRE, and who was going to go fishing later that day.

Danny and Tom exchanged a look, and he knew before he even saw the uniforms that it had to be the military.

"FEMA," Danny whispered. She crouched down and peeked out from behind a rock. Jesper gave her a questioning look.

"The sign!" she insisted. "They have a FEMA sign on the barricade."

Tom moved up next to her to get a better look, and sure enough, there was a large white sign with black lettering, just like the one at FEMA Shelter M3.

"Patterson didn't say anything about a sign," Jesper grumbled. "It must be new."

Tom stood and offered Danny a hand. Pulling her easily to her feet, he then raised a finger to his mouth before carefully backing away. The last thing they needed was another all-inclusive stay with the US military.

Before they made it back to where they'd left the road, the helicopter they'd heard approaching for the past several minutes finally swooped down into view, flying low over the roadblock. Dropping to his knees, Tom watched as it continued up the road before veering sharply to the left, toward the churning clouds.

"Do you think they saw us?" Danny gasped, watching the helicopter closely as it moved away.

Jesper was up and walking so fast, that he was nearly running when his feet hit the pavement of the road. "Not us," he huffed, looking back over his shoulder. "But I'd be willing to wager they saw our eight horses gathered just up the road."

"You don't need to go any further with us," Tom said as the three of them fell into a steady gait. "The map you drew of the Miner's Trail is detailed enough. It should be easy for me to find where it meets up with US Route 12."

"It doesn't get used much," Jesper answered, not trying to talk Tom out of starting on the trail without him. "But after more than a century of running cattle on that track, the Earth pretty much gave up her fight to reclaim it."

Tom knew exactly what the rancher meant. He'd been on enough of these types of trails that he was confident in his ability to stay on it. It stirred a poignant memory of the nights he spent under the stars with his dad, on the other end of the same trail. He was raised in the mountains surrounding Mercy, and that included countless rides. He might not have participated in an actual cattle drive, but he'd heard the stories while out on hunting trips, or when exploring and learning to live off the land.

Tom paused for a moment as they drew near the horses and fought to control his emotions. He didn't know if it was yet another side effect of the concussion, or maybe he was simply starting to lose it, but he had a sudden, overwhelming sense of loss.

"Tom?"

He was surprised by the hand on his arm, and turned to find Danny studying him, a worried look on her face. A face full of fading bruises and cuts, some of which he had put there himself.

"Are you okay? Is it another headache?" Danny's grip on his arm tightened and Tom resisted the urge to place his own over top of it. Instead, he pulled away and offered a forced smile.

"I will be," Tom said, deciding to be honest. Looking at Sam and Ethan, who were busy saying goodbye to Jesper and his men, the crease between his brows deepened. Danny was still watching him and so Tom met her gaze, holding it for a moment in what was perhaps the most open exchange they'd shared yet. "First, I have to get home."

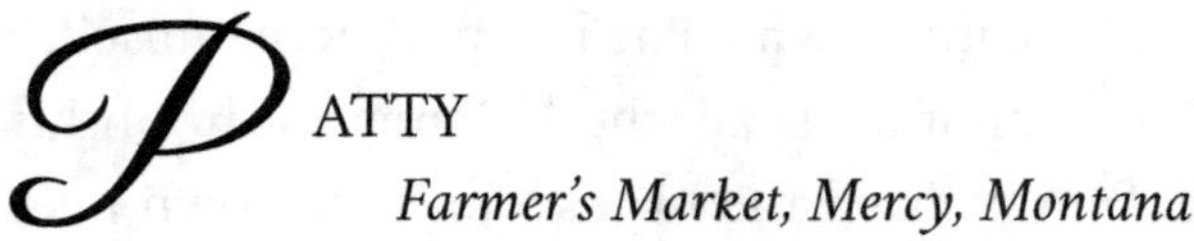PATTY

Farmer's Market, Mercy, Montana

PATTY SAT her basket of apples down with a loud huff. Straightening slowly, she rubbed at a sore shoulder while taking in the latest changes at the market. The sound of hammers working on the final touches for the covered stands was a melody she found comforting. There were ten spaces, in two rows, one down either side of the road. It left a large aisle in the middle big enough for horses and the carriage to pass through.

"Good morning, Mayor!" a woman called out as she walked by, a baby on one hip and a bag of potatoes on the other.

Patty waved in response, trying to remember the girl's name and failing. She'd always been horrible at recalling names and had tried to use it as an excuse to get out of the last election, claiming she could never pass as a politician because of it.

Although it was still early, there were at least a couple dozen people at the market. Children as well as chickens ran around under foot, and Patty was pretty sure she might have heard a pig. She would need to speak with Sandy about getting some pens set up in addition to the fruit stands. The bartering system was a huge success and seemed to be quite popular with everyone she'd spoken to. There had been some fear that it would lead to arguments in regard to what was a fair trade, but so far, the people of Mercy were able to successfully negotiate with little intervention from law enforcement.

The police. Patty sighed. It was another one of the many items on her to-do list for the day. She had a meeting with Sheriff Waters that afternoon to discuss his ongoing shortage. With the increase in guards stationed at both ends of town, it left only two officers available at any given time, even with the volunteers. While the crime rate in Mercy wasn't a concern, just like before the flashpoint, law enforcement handled much more than straightforward criminal activity. With over six hundred residents, there were frequent domestic disputes, fights, drunken brawls, and random citizen complaints. Even a dog attack occurred the night before that left one man with a nasty bite, a dead dog, and an owner that wanted revenge.

While Patty went about adding her apples to the fruit stand, she frowned as she thought about the irony of it all. Here they were, in the middle of what was most likely the end of the world as they knew it, and she was going to spend her afternoon trying to figure out how to settle personality conflicts and neighbor disagreements. "Life must go on," she muttered, taking a bite out of an especially sweet-looking Honeycrisp.

"You look like you could use a drink," a familiar voice called out from close by, and Patty paused before taking a second mouthful of apple.

Turning, she confirmed that a man named Alan was leaning

in the open door of his bar, The Last Stop. She frowned. He was holding what looked suspiciously like a glass of beer. He stepped aside as two men walked past him to go inside, despite the early hour.

"You're open for business?" Patty asked, moving closer so they didn't have to shout at each other.

"I was never really closed," Alan confirmed, raising the glass toward her. "Figuring out how to finish my last batch of beer didn't take much. The still was a little trickier, but I got some recruits to help with that. Took ten days to get my first brew out."

"Moonshine?" Patty asked, not really wanting to know the answer. "I think I'll pass." Mentally adding the topic to her list of interesting things to discuss with the sheriff, she broke off the conversation before she said something that would upset Alan. He was a long-standing friend of Caleb's, and she knew he was a good guy. It just bothered her that able-bodied people were working on concocting alcohol when there was so much else that needed to be done.

Smiling absently at people as she walked back through the market, Patty focused instead on their accomplishments. In spite of what Gary would have everyone believe, they'd come a very long way in only fifteen days. As she approached City Hall, the aromatic smoke rising from the central park area helped bolster that sentiment.

Entering the city center, Patty scanned the crowd and easily picked out her husband. He was hauling a stack of wood, and was already sweating through his work clothes. He'd been busy smoking the rest of the steer and his team had been at it all night. Without any way to refrigerate the beef, they had to move fast. Managing the large smoker while keeping it at a steady hundred and sixty-five degrees wasn't easy.

"How's it going?" Patty asked when she caught Caleb's eye.

Dropping the wood on the ground next to the smoker, he flashed a huge smile at her. Pulling a piece of leathery meat from the front pocket of his shirt, he offered it to her. "Try some for yourself and let me know what you think."

What was it with men offering her questionable products that morning? Hesitating only briefly, Patty accepted the small rubbery piece of jerky. After the first bite, she began nodding her head and happily ate the rest. "It's amazing, Caleb. How much do you think we'll end up with?"

His smile fading, Caleb crossed his arms over his chest. "Not enough to get through the winter. Even if we were to manage to keep this pace up in the coming weeks, we're going to have to start working on other methods to store different types of food."

Patty had already guessed what the answer would be. Without a way to stockpile perishables, they were severely restricted in what they could save. While they had several sources of fresh eggs and cows' milk, it simply wasn't enough for the whole town. In time, if done properly, they could increase their herds and expand the gardens. The problem was that they didn't have time, and there was no way to call a time-out. Though it was barely the month of July, Patty was already dreading the winter. She had a feeling they'd all be a lot leaner come next spring.

Patty shivered at the thought, and then realized that it was also due to a cold breeze that had suddenly kicked up. She searched for the source of the shift and wasn't surprised by the brewing clouds to the south of the valley. The weather was another concern. It was already unseasonably cooler, especially at night. And it wasn't the first time that a storm had been visible on the horizon, though so far, it had either headed to the west or dissipated.

"Feels like this one might decide to come for a visit," Caleb said, looking up at the sky with concern. "That'll make running this smoker all the harder. I'd better go get some more wood cut and stacked where it'll stay dry, just in case."

Patty was going to try and steal a kiss from her husband before he could get away, but she was interrupted by the sound of a horse running into the center at full speed. Alarmed, Patty sought out the source, knowing instinctively that it wouldn't be something good.

"Patty!" It was Melissa shouting her name, and the doctor sounded frantic.

Her stomach turning cold with fear that the deadly infection must have returned, Patty pushed past Caleb and ran to where Melissa was still sitting on her horse. Her hair was loose and wild-looking and her face was ashen.

"What's happened?" Patty shouted, looking behind Melissa to see if anyone was with her, but she appeared to be alone.

"There's been an accident," Melissa barked, already turning her horse around. "I'm on my way there. It's the wagon. It rolled on the way down the hill from the spring. It's bad, Patty. We need some men and horses to help lift things, and…"

Though Patty felt some relief that it wasn't cholera, the loss of the wagon would be a devastating blow. Hopefully, they'd be able to salvage it. She realized Melissa was still staring at her, looking dazed. "Melissa, what is it?" she pressed.

"I was told that there are four people injured, and two of them are already dead. Crushed under the water tank."

Patty closed her eyes briefly and then began to move to where her horse was tethered. Caleb was already ahead of her, and calling out to some other men to follow them. They'd deal with it. The same way they'd faced and overcome every other setback along the way. It was why the people of Mercy would thrive where others floundered. Gritting her teeth, Patty walked faster, resolute in her determination.

"Patty!" Melissa shouted again.

Not understanding why her friend insisted on talking more when they clearly needed to hurry, Patty looked back with some irritation. "What?"

Melissa's eyes were filling with tears. "I'm going to need your help more than ever, because Trevor was on the wagon."

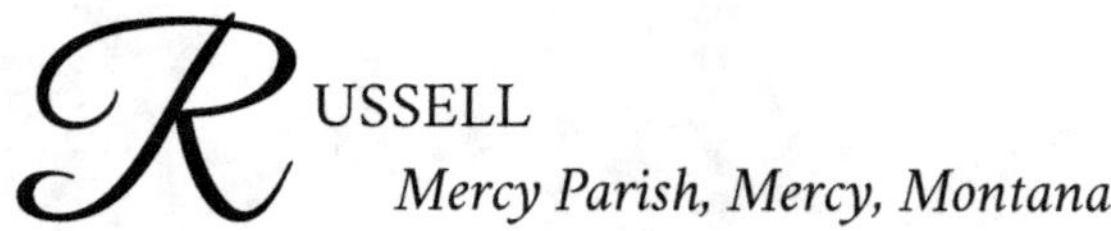

CHAPTER 12

RUSSELL
Mercy Parish, Mercy, Montana

RUSSELL SAT at the back of the church with his head bowed in supposed prayer. He'd been holding the painful position for nearly an hour while Father White went through his rituals, in preparation for the evening mass.

Russell was raised Catholic, so he'd had no problem determining which religion Father White practiced, based only on his vestments. It played perfectly into his plans. While attending his theology courses, he wrote a paper on the Episcopalian faith, which included how one could become a priest. As a result, Russell knew not only what was expected from an Episcopalian priest, but also what schools existed and where they were located, as well as the length it took to achieve the position. By claiming that particular faith, he hoped to circumvent any pointed questions that might call his bluff.

So far, there hadn't been an inquisition. In fact, Father White was going out of his way to avoid him. Russell opened an eye and peeked to see where the grumpy old codger was at. The room appeared empty. Opening both eyes, he looked around and confirmed that he was alone. The alter was set, candles were lit, and as he stood on stiffened knees, a side door opened and a plump, middle-aged woman wandered inside.

"Oh!" she gasped, a hand going to her throat. "Is Father White here? I'm Madeline, the pianist."

Russell beamed at Madeline and was rewarded by an instant flush to her cheeks. "It's so nice to meet you. I'm Father Rogers." He gestured to his dirty jeans and plain shirt. "You'll have to forgive my attire. I've been on the road for some days and just arrived."

"You're the pastor from Wyoming!" Madeline said with enthusiasm as she shuffled amongst the pews, making her way toward him. "We're thrilled to have another pastor here in Mercy."

Russell accepted her outstretched hand when she finally reached him and shook it eagerly. "Guilty as charged," he teased. "But I'm afraid my journey and intent have likely been exaggerated. I'm here only as a guest. To be honest with you, Madeline," he added, leaning close enough for her to smell the cologne he'd put on that morning. "My faith has come under attack. During these end days I join the people of Mercy as nothing more than a weak man, seeking redemption."

Madeline was still holding his hand, and she covered it with her other one before lifting it towards her chest like a maiden seeking the blessing of her king. "Oh, Father Rogers, I implore you to share your wisdom with this parish. We need to hear the words of someone who recognizes the trying times we're facing and how it can alter our views of what faith means to us."

"Ahem." From behind them, Father White very loudly cleared his throat.

Wincing, Russell pulled his hand out from Madeline's grasp and offered her a conspiratorial wink before turning to face the priest. "Father. I've had the joy of meeting your pianist. Do you have any other musicians participate in your services?" Already knowing what the answer was, Russell enjoyed the expected rise he got from the old man.

"Certainly not!" Father White spat. "Mercy is an orthodox parish, Father Rogers. While you may have allowed a band to lead your congregation onto whatever path you chose, we will have nothing of the sort here. Let us be clear on that."

"My apologies, Father," Russell purred while barely hiding his smile. At least he'd gotten the man to say more than one sentence. Mayor Patty had brought Russell to the apartment behind the church the night before, after the barbeque. He hadn't even met Father White until late that morning when they'd exchanged nothing more than formal introductions. Since Russell was volunteered by Patty to fish all afternoon, it had been easy to stay under the other man's radar.

Madeline, sensing the tension, made a quick departure. Soon, the church was full of hymnal music. Russell sincerely hoped Father White wouldn't quiz him on any of the sung prayers, since many of them were shared between the denominations. Music wasn't something Russell had ever gotten into, nor payed attention to.

"What seminary did you attend?"

Russell raised an eyebrow at Father White, intrigued by his guile. "I was blessed with the opportunity to go to Berkeley Divinity School at Yale," Russell answered without any hesitation. "A beautiful campus. Although that was many years ago, I must say, and quite a lot has changed over the past decade."

Father White grunted before moving to open the front doors. Russell followed, and watched as the elderly man painstakingly updated the church service marquee board, located near the sweeping stone steps.

"I was a postulant for nearly a year," Russell offered while handing the priest a letter he needed. "I confess I was a bit eager in my younger years and had more confidence than was warranted."

"A trait not uncommon among those seeking to be ordained," Father White mumbled. It wasn't much, but Russell still considered it progress.

He was rather enjoying his time with the old priest. The man was still sharp, in spite of his years, and had the same cunning as the Catholic minister Russell grew up with. For years, Russell attended Sunday mass with his mother and younger brother. It was during some of the more poignant sermons that he came to understand how he was different from everyone else. It was tempting to believe he'd been called into existence to serve a higher being, but Russell saw beyond that veil. The tapestry he was woven into wasn't so simple as good and evil or right and wrong. His was a thread that, if pulled, revealed an intricate path capable of either unraveling the fabric or holding it all together.

Russell was ten when their pastor caught him in the alley behind the church, mutilating a cat. When confronted, instead of being ashamed and trying to run away, he had giggled. Apparently, that left quite an impression, because he was later subjected to extreme prayer sessions, held in his attic room, the air heavy with the scent of frankincense.

The distant notes of the organ could almost be mistaken for the tune of "Edelweiss", if Russell closed his eyes and didn't think too hard about it. The smell of burning candles wafted through the air and the atmosphere was heavy with a looming storm. Almost like the oppressive, muggy confines of the attic.

"Father Rogers. Are you okay?"

Russell jumped at the nearness of the priest, and for a

moment, only a brief fraction of a second, his eyes dropped the mask he spent his life behind.

Father White took a step back. He fumbled with the letters still clasped between his fingers, and his discomfort was almost comical.

Before Russell had a chance to attempt and smooth things over, two horses came galloping down the street. The church was on the northwest edge of town and was the last building on the road, so it was obvious where they were heading. Russell didn't think it was normal for the congregation to rush to mass in such a manner, so he followed after Father White to go greet them.

Two men Russell had never seen before reined their mounts in at the last moment, kicking up dust on the pastor's white robes. Lightning jabbed at the sky behind them as one of them dismounted, his face distorted with grief. "Father, we need you to come with us to the clinic."

"Is it the—"

"No," the man still seated on his horse interrupted. "Not the cholera. There was an accident with the wagon."

"It took us several hours to get everyone out of the wreckage and to the clinic," the man standing in front of Father White explained, his voice strained. He glanced over at Russell. "You the new priest?"

Russell nodded without thinking much about it, but was answered by a sharp look from Father White.

"Good," the man continued, turning his attention back again to Father White. "We can use you both for the last rites."

CHAPTER 13

JAMES
      Master Sergeant, US Marines, 1st Force Recon-
naissance
Cheyenne Mountain, Colorado

THE TICKING of the clock seemed abnormally loud. James refused to look at it, and it took all of his self-control not to shift uncomfortably in the leather chair. He hadn't noticed the *tick-tick-tick* of the old-style mechanism the last time he'd been in General Montgomery's office, but it was probably because he'd been distracted. Or, perhaps the air units that shut off as he entered had been running during the past meeting, drowning the smaller noise out.

More than likely, it was because the general was staring silently at James. Montgomery's attention hadn't wavered for a good two minutes, so that James became acutely aware of everything around them. Such as a fluorescent light over the table in the room behind him that was flickering. There was also a low, resonant vibration in the granite floor that James could feel in his feet, and a piece of red yarn had come loose from a tack on the general's giant map. It hung just inside James's view and was moving slightly from a current of air he couldn't feel.

He was having a hard time determining the mood of the general, which James found very disconcerting. He was normally an excellent judge of people and their demeanors. Montgomery was certainly paler since he'd last seen him four days earlier. He might have even lost a few pounds, though his starched uniform made it difficult to tell. He was perfectly still, aside from the index finger of his left hand, which was making small, quick movements on top of the desk, almost like he was scratching at the wood.

Unable to stop himself, James shifted his eyes to look more closely at the motion. Montgomery's hand froze and he cleared his throat, leading James to believe the general hadn't even been aware he was doing it.

"I didn't realize that 1ˢᵗ Force Reconnaissance had a problem following orders." The general's voice was level and free of irritation, but the allegation was clear nonetheless.

"Sir?" James was honestly surprised by the remark.

"I thought it was made clear that there were to be no other packages taken with the asset."

James stared at General Montgomery for a moment as he processed the statement. He had an internal battle between soldier and father as he grasped that the little girl was being referred to in such a manner. "The child is the doctor's granddaughter," James said carefully, being sure not to allow any emotions to show. "I… used her as leverage, sir, to prevent an unnecessary conflict."

Montgomery picked up a pen and began tapping it, his eyes narrowing. "Yes. I read the report. I'm aware of your justifications, and while I can appreciate a certain level of ingenuity in the field, I still expect you to adhere to standing orders. They are *not* a guideline. I need to make sure you're clear on that before you leave on your next mission."

"Crystal." James noticed the general's eyes narrowing further. "Sir."

"Have you been apprised of the next assignment?" Montgomery slid a folder across his desk as he spoke, and then tapped it once, lightly.

James looked down at the plain manila folder with some uneasiness. "Only that we leave before dawn." When it became clear that he was meant to take it, he begrudgingly picked it up. There was only one sheet of paper inside. That was all he needed.

Montgomery watched as James frowned down at the document. "The asset made contact some days ago, but as of yet, their location has not been confirmed. You're being sent to their residence. Is that going to be a problem, Sergeant?"

James shifted in the chair and then leaned forward on one knee, holding the folder out towards the general. "What happens to the assets, sir?"

Montgomery leaned back with an expression that suggested he finally got the reaction he was expecting. Slapping his hands dramatically on the arms of his chair, the general pushed himself up and walked out from behind the grand desk. "Normally, that isn't a question I would answer, but in your case I'm willing to make an exception." Turning away from James, he began to pace in front of the world map.

James watched the older man carefully, bothered by the image of the ornately-clad commander taking measured steps across the room. The looming image of marked destruction as a backdrop was unsettling, rather than motivating. James didn't see much hope on that map, and his feelings for the general were troubled. Normally, he wouldn't bother to worry over how he did or didn't feel about a commander, but since this commander was the man leading what was left of their country…it mattered.

"Sergeant, the men and woman on the Survivor's List have been deemed the greatest minds of our nation," Montgomery began, pausing in his march. "Doctors, leaders, teachers, and scientists in various fields. They are the key to rebuilding. With their knowledge and ingenuity, we can and will work our way back from the brink of complete destruction. They will be treated as a precious commodity." Moving back to his desk, he stopped in front of James. "I can, however, understand your misgivings."

James stood, noting how the general didn't take a step back as most men would. "Not at all, sir. Tomorrow's mission will be handled the same as any other."

General Montgomery reached out slowly and took ahold of the folder, setting it back pointedly on the desk. "Make sure that it is. No matter who the asset is."

CHAPTER 14

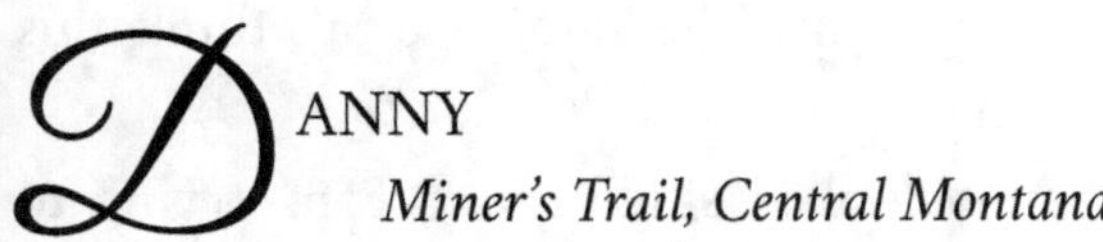

ANNY
Miner's Trail, Central Montana

LIGHTNING CRACKLED overhead and the hair on the back of Danny's arms rose. She had a very bad feeling that they were about to bear the full brunt of the storm they'd been eyeing for more than a day.

"What's with the orange lightning?" Ethan asked Sam as the two of them rode side by side, behind Danny. Tom was leading the way, and had been since they'd started out on the Miner's Trail.

"My guess is it has to do with the chemical changes in the atmosphere I was telling you about," Sam explained, gazing up at the sky.

"Oxides?" Ethan said, sounding uncertain.

"Essentially," Sam replied. He started getting into more detail about chemical compounds and Danny stopped listening. It was all fascinating up to a point, but she was well over her initial curiosity when it came to the upper atmosphere.

Spurring her horse on, Danny took advantage of the flatter span of trail they were currently on to move up next to Tom. She chuckled when she saw how Grace lay sprawled across Lily's shoulders, her head nestled against Tom's thigh, sound asleep.

"How do you do that?" Danny asked, raising an eyebrow at Tom.

He did his best to look innocent. "Do what?"

"Get a dog who can hardly sit still long enough to be petted, to fall asleep on the back of a horse?" Danny said playfully. "You must be a dog whisperer, as well as a horse and cattle whisperer."

Tom shrugged and then rested a hand on Lily's neck. "I think it's as much the horse as it is me," he said. "I don't think this would happen if I rode Tango."

Laughing lightly, Danny looked sideways at Tom, trying to study his features without being too obvious. The bruising and swelling had healed to the point that he wasn't quite so scary looking, and she might even describe him as ruggedly good looking. It was his unusual green eyes that intrigued her the most. Danny knew he was intelligent, and when he turned his full attention on her, it was like he could read her mind, sometimes.

Tom turned his head then and caught her staring, so she tried to cover it up with a question. "I've been wondering..."

"Yeah?" Tom smiled crookedly at her while absently petting Grace.

"Between the Duke and Miller ranches, whose is bigger?"

Tom looked somewhat surprised by her question, and seemed happy to talk about his ranch. "We have over five thousand acres and close to a thousand head of cattle," he said with some pride.

Danny tried to pretend like she knew what that meant. "So... yours is the biggest?"

Tom laughed. "Yeah, Duke's is about half the size of our operation, although his pastures are underused, so they could take on more."

Danny recalled the men's parting conversation that morning, and how they were talking about keeping in touch and possibly setting up some trades. After watching the two of the men interact for two days, she felt she had a greater understanding of the camaraderie the rancher community shared.

"So then how about the *blue* lightning?" Ethan's voice rose as his conversation with Sam became more animated. Danny was used to the friendly banter the two often shared, and she envied it to a certain degree.

Ethan's question was punctuated by a blinding flash of intense bluish light, visible even though it was still the middle of the afternoon. Earth-shaking thunder followed it, and then a silence so deep that Tom stopped Lilly.

The woods the trail had taken them through was a mixture of open plains interspersed with steeper, rocky glades. As Danny tried to interpret the heaviness that seemed to accompany the silence, she was thankful that the current landscape was at least relatively flat, although heavily wooded. After the morning fog burned off, the temperatures reached a high of around eighty, but an unusual humidity made it feel like they were in a sauna. Tugging at her sticky T-shirt, Danny couldn't shake the feeling that something malevolent was about to be released, and they were right in its path.

Twisting in his saddle, Tom looked back at Danny first, and then Sam and Ethan. They were all spooked. He looked up, and Danny followed his gaze. A bizarre display of what Sam called mammatus clouds hung overhead, huge drooping protrusions that reminded Danny of being underwater. The comparison might not be too far from accurate.

There was a perceptible shift in the temperature, a sudden plunge followed by a wind blowing from the opposite direction of the storm. As the wind increased, it began to howl around them, and then abruptly stopped, thunder rumbling in its wake.

Grace lifted her head and whined before twisting around and leaping off of Lily's back. Barking once, she started to run up the trail.

"I think Grace has the right idea," Sam said nervously. "Let's get out of here."

None of them needed any more encouragement and they took off at a challenging pace. Danny winced as she bounced in the saddle, knowing she was going to pay for all of the hard riding they'd already done that day. She would have thought that after more than a week there would come a point where it wouldn't hurt anymore. However, if that were the case, she apparently hadn't achieved enough experience to call herself a cowgirl yet.

"State Route 12 shouldn't be more than a few miles away," Tom called back. "This trail puts out at a campground. Maybe we can find some shelter there before the storm breaks loose."

Danny tried to remember the map Tom had showed her when they stopped earlier for lunch. No matter how much she recalled, it still didn't make a whole lot of sense. She knew they'd crossed Highway 90 a few hours earlier, so that gave Danny a better grasp of where they were, geographically speaking. While it was a stretch of road she wasn't necessarily familiar with, just knowing they were momentarily standing on a highway she had driven on so often brought a certain level of comfort. Of course, once they'd disappeared back into the trees she may as well have been on the moon.

Sam was trying to shout something in response, but his words were lost in the wind. It was then that the sky literally split open and a wall of water was unleashed.

Danny gasped as the cool rain hit her face with alarming force, instantly soaking her clothes. Her vision blurred, and her horse must have been blinded too, because she faltered and then slowed to a walk.

The wind howled again, an eerie sound unlike anything Danny had ever heard before. She began to shiver, and it was in that moment that she realized how people died from exposure in the mountains. She didn't know what to do except hold on and keep moving, so long as Tom didn't stop in front of her. She could still see him, or rather, his form moving in the premature darkness. It was like the rain had brought the very clouds down with it, to encase them in a surreal landscape that didn't exist only moments before.

"Dad!" Ethan shouted from somewhere close, and Danny strained to see him through the torrential onslaught.

"Keep moving!" Tom replied, his voice muffled.

As abruptly as the rain had started, it disappeared, leaving Danny blinking rapidly in the aftermath. A mosaic of dark shadows glided over them and through the clearing they were in. The wind shifted again, intensifying at the same time.

"What's happening?" Danny cried. She knew her voice was shaking, but she didn't care at that moment about being brave. The trail had turned to mud as the massive amount of rain pooled in any flat area, and her horse slipped, threatening to unseat her. Leaves and pine needles swirled around them, engaged in some form of dance normally reserved for an audience of fairies.

Sam's horse came alongside her, and Danny could see that her friend's head was turned up to the sky. He looked around almost frantically, and the hairs on her arms stood once again.

"I've never seen a twister out here," Sam shouted to anyone who could hear him. "But this is certainly a storm cell capable of producing one."

"A tornado!" Danny repeated, flinching as another wild crack of lightning lit the trees around them. That one was orange and she briefly understood Ethan's interest in how the colors were variable.

A new sound began to develop under the roar of the wind, a plopping or ticking, like pebbles thrown against a window. Then, Danny felt the first sting as a sizeable piece of ice hit her bare arm. "Hail!" she moaned. Normally, she enjoyed a good storm and would often sit out on the roof of the fire station as the lightning developed. However, there was nothing normal about what they were experiencing, including the hail. It wasn't your typical pea-sized pellets, but huge chunks about half the size of a golf ball.

"Ouch!" Danny ducked as another struck her back, though there was nowhere to hide.

"We need to get off the horses!" Sam yelled, already stopped and sliding out of his saddle. "Tom! We've got to find some shelter!"

Danny didn't think it was possible, but the wind continued to grow in strength. The trees groaned under the strain as the tops bent over and sizeable branches crashed to the ground. One clawed at her cheek, compelling Danny to follow Sam's instructions. Yelping in pain, she threw an arm over her head in vain as she jumped to the ground.

"We're close to the campground." Tom suddenly appeared next to Danny, and she was relieved to see he was holding Grace protectively in his arms. He led the way into the trees next to the trail, though they didn't offer much protection. "The cliff Jesper told me about is just ahead." Tom winced as a piece of ice bounced off his shoulder and he looked angry about it rather than concerned. Danny knew him well enough to figure he was already chastising himself for not going faster, or for taking too long for lunch. He always managed to find a way to blame himself for the things that went wrong, even when it was Mother Nature.

"Where's Ethan?" Tom shouted.

A frenzied whinny drew their attention back to the trail, and Danny turned to see Ethan struggling to control Tango as he reared up in fright. She reached out to take Grace from Tom without him asking, and then watched as he raced out into the storm. Danny stood helpless, her hair whipping across her face and ice tearing at her arms.

Before Tom could reach his son, there was a horrendous splintering sound, and dread filled Danny as she realized it was a falling tree that blocked them both from view.

CHAPTER 15

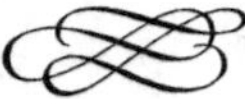

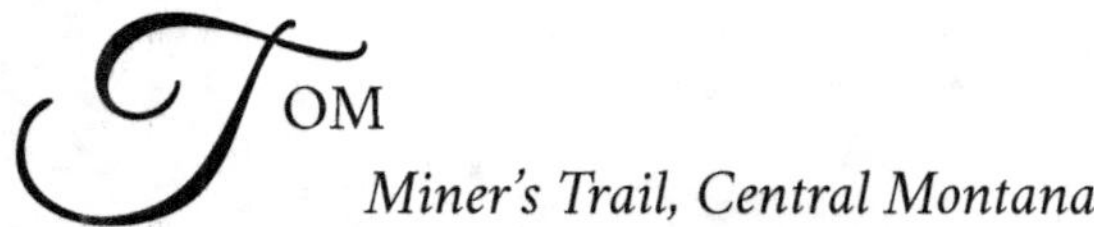

TOM

Miner's Trail, Central Montana

THE BLUR of movement confused Tom for a moment, until the sound of the splintering wood reached him. Desperately throwing his arms over his head, he leapt to where he'd last seen Ethan.

He was met by a wall of foliage that clawed at him, pushing him back and pressing him into the ground at the same time. With the howling wind and blinding rain, Tom felt like he'd been trapped in the churning bowels of the earth.

"Ethan!" Tom shouted, ignoring the new flashes of pain in his back and right thigh. He was still moving forward. All that mattered was getting to his son.

Pushing aside a final branch, Tom broke loose from the fallen cedar tree and staggered out into what remained of the clearing. He splashed through pooling water as the hail turned back to rain. Wiping it from his eyes, he searched for a sign of Ethan.

Tango was standing nearby, his ears back, pawing at the ground and turning it to mud.

"Ethan!" Tom yelled again, his voice sounding more frantic, even to himself.

"Dad, I'm okay!" Ethan's voice was faint but close by. "I…I think I'm okay, but I can't really move."

"Tom!" Danny called.

Tom looked up to see Danny and Sam running around the massive mound of fresh dirt the fallen tree had uprooted. He waved a hand at them, unsure if they could see him through all of the branches. "We're over here!"

When Danny reached him, he saw that her arms and neck were peppered with red welts from the hail, and there was a large, raw scratch across her cheek. "Where's Ethan?" Her eyes were wide with fear, and she had to shout to be heard over the wind.

Tom pointed at the cedar and shook his head. "In there, somewhere. Sam, can you get your flashlight?"

Sam didn't even acknowledge the request before he ran away, and Tom turned back to Danny. "Help me."

Nodding silently, she moved up next to him and together, they began pushing through the limbs, heavy with long cedar boughs. "You're bleeding," she said, leaning in close so he could hear her. When he stared at her uncomprehendingly, she paused long enough to pull the cloth headband from her hair. Using it like a rag, she wiped the blood from his right eye and then pressed it, hard, against the wound on his forehead that he'd re-opened.

"I'm fine," he protested, trying to pull away.

"Hold on!" Grabbing his forearm, she kept the compress in place for another ten seconds. Pulling the cloth back slightly, she was satisfied enough then to let him go.

"Here!" Sam was back with the flashlight, and held it out to

Tom. Racked by a coughing fit, Sam stepped back and then sat down hard on the wet ground.

"Where's your inhaler?" Danny demanded.

Tom snapped the light on as the two of them talked, and he turned back to the tree. He knew Danny would take care of Sam. Ethan was still his main priority, but the branches seemed impenetrable.

"I'm here, Dad!"

Tom could hear his son calling to him, but couldn't see how to get any closer to where he was nestled under the vegetation. The tree was simply too gigantic to even think about moving.

Woof! Woof!

"Grace!" Spinning around, Tom saw the retriever was running back and forth between Danny, Tango, and the edge of the tree. "Grace! Find Ethan!" Tom had no idea if the dog would understand the command, but she seemed to respond to it. Whining, she ran faster, and started to paw at the ground.

"Find Ethan, Grace!" Danny also shouted. She was kneeling down next to Sam, helping him with his inhaler. The rain was so heavy that Tom had to blink against it, and his vision blurred.

Grace barked again, this time with more excitement, and then she lunged in between the branches. Within a few minutes, the pitch of her bark increased and she almost sounded like she was being tortured.

"Good girl!" Ethan shouted, his voice barely audible over the wind, rain, and barking. "She found me!"

Tom looked back at Danny to discover that she was gone. Sam was trying to stand, the inhaler still in his hand. "Sit back down, Sam," he ordered.

Danny reappeared around the end of the tree again, and she held something in both of her hands. As she ran toward him, Tom realized she had the axes. "Here," she ordered, thrusting one at him. "Let's get to work."

After an hour of clearing away the largest of the branches from that section of the tree, they finally exposed where Grace was furiously digging in the mud. Tom dropped to his knees next to her and shone the flashlight into the cluster of boughs. "Ethan, you still doing okay? We'll have you out in a minute."

The whites of Ethan's eyes shone bright in the flashlight, and his teeth flashed when he smiled. "My arm just hurts a little. I'll bet I'm a lot drier than you guys!"

Laughing, Danny pushed in next to Tom, pulling at the cedar with her bare hands to make a larger opening. "What's got you trapped?" she asked, already trying to work through the problem.

"I think I could push my way through most of this," Ethan answered. "Except there's one bigger branch laying across my back. The ground was soft enough that I don't think it really hurt me, but I can't wiggle out from under it. Guess my butt's too big."

Tom smiled back. It was a good sign he was joking about it. "Hold on."

Standing, he reached out and pulled Danny to her feet. They were both covered with scratches from pushing through the cedar branches, and mud was caked onto almost every visible surface. "Let's find that branch."

Working their way back from where they found Ethan, they were able to locate what they thought was the largest of the branches pinning him down. It was difficult to swing the ax effectively in the confined space, and Tom was grateful when Danny joined him on the opposite side. It was painstaking work, but together they managed to finally cut through it.

"That was it!" Ethan shouted, and Tom could hear him thrashing around.

Going back to where Grace was still digging, he reached in and was finally able to grasp Ethan's hand. Grunting with the effort, he dug his heels in and leaned back, pulling with all of his strength.

First one arm, and then the other came out into the open space they'd created. Danny got down on her hands and knees and grabbed Ethan's belt, using it like a rope to help work the rest of his body free.

"Oomph!" Ethan gasped as Grace lunged onto his chest and began to enthusiastically lick the mud from his face.

Tom hooked him under the armpits and lifted Ethan to his feet. It had been awhile since he'd tried to pick his son up, and Tom realized he was almost the size of a man. Staring at the back of his child's head, the one that reached above his chin, he was forced to admit Ethan wasn't a child anymore. Tom rested his hands on Ethan's shoulders and then turned him around. Holding him at arm's length, he tried to determine if there were any serious injuries, but all he saw was mud.

"I'm okay, Dad." Even under the extreme conditions, Ethan still managed to sound put out by the concern.

"This looks like it might hurt a little." Danny was attempting to get a closer look at an obvious abrasion on his upper right arm.

Rolling his shoulder, Ethan winced when he straightened his arm out. "Yeah, it's sore, but I can still move it okay. No biggie."

"We were all lucky," Sam said as he ducked under one branch and pushed aside another. He coughed and then pointed up at the sky. "Looks like the worst of the storm passed, and the horses are okay," he added.

Tom noticed it had brightened considerably and the rain was even tolerable. The wind still kicked up occasionally with thirty to forty-mile-per-hour gusts, but the sustained breeze was much less. "We should get moving, then. We still have a few hours of daylight left."

"Whoa!" Danny urged, stepping in front of him. "Don't you think Ethan and Sam could use a rest? Maybe we should stay here for tonight and use this tree for a shelter."

Tom was rattled after the storm and with how close he'd come to losing his son. He was emotionally charged and on edge, so while he managed not to say the first thing that came to mind, he knew he didn't keep it from his face. Danny frowned at him and took a full step back. Sighing, Tom ran a hand through his hair, realizing he'd lost his cowboy hat at some point. "Look," he finally said, knowing he wasn't going to do a good job of placating her. "We can cover another twenty miles tonight. It could make the difference between getting to Mercy in two days or three."

"I said I'm fine," Ethan interjected. He was kneeling down in the mud with Grace and had finally managed to calm the dog.

Danny crossed her arms over her chest, and Tom knew he was in trouble. "The storm caused a bronchial reaction in Sam. Either the cold or something in the air, but I don't think he should travel."

"Danny," Sam said. "I appreciate your concern, but do you really think it will make a difference? Since the storm is letting up, this might be the best chance we have to travel in the next couple of days. We have no idea what the forecast is."

Tom had always envied how easily the older man communicated with Danny, and he watched as the two of them had a calm, rational conversation. In the end, Danny agreed to two more hours of riding, and they'd stop immediately if his breathing got any worse.

As Tom put his ax back on the packhorse, he resisted the urge to take the map out again. It wasn't waterproof and although they were close to where the old trail ended and the one he was familiar with began, he didn't want to take any chances with it.

"Why does the rain taste weird?" Ethan asked. He was already back on Tango, and Tom saw that he was favoring his right arm by cradling it against his chest.

"What do you mean?" Tom licked at his lips. It was hardly raining anymore, but he was still covered in it.

Ethan shrugged. "I dunno…like, sour or something."

"I figured it was running out of my hair, and I just need to take a shower," Danny offered with a grin. Tom was glad to see her smiling again, though she hadn't said much to him as they prepared the horses.

Sam gave Ethan and Danny an odd look, and then to Tom's surprise, licked his arm. He frowned.

"What is it?" Tom asked.

Sam licked his other arm and then smacked his lips, his thick brows drawing together in consternation. "It tastes like metal."

"Okay…" Tom said slowly, not liking the way Sam was looking around at the trees and then the sky. He followed his gaze and saw that the bulk of the monster storm cell had passed over, and was moving to the north, toward Mercy.

"Nitric acid," Sam said, as if that explained everything.

"Acid?" Danny repeated. "You've got to be kidding me."

"I'm afraid I'm not." Sam licked his arm again.

"Stop!" Danny said, moving closer to him. "If it's acid, isn't it dangerous?"

Sam shook his head and then waved a hand up at the sky. "It's part of the same process that stripped the ozone layer and is producing these storms. The conversion of nitrogen and oxygen into oxides. The nitrous oxide rises and then combines with other chemicals to produce the acid rain. But it shouldn't be harmful to us directly," he added as an afterthought.

"Are you sure?" Ethan asked, not looking convinced.

"You can swim in acid rain without any immediate effects," Sam replied. "It's a slight PH difference, although the fact that we can taste it indicates it must be at a PH around five, at the most."

Tom had no idea what that meant, but he was relieved their skin wasn't going to melt off. "Can we drink it?"

Sam rubbed at his chin. "My understanding of it is that yes, we could, but I wouldn't recommend it long-term. It could lead to...complications. No, the greatest impact will be to the lakes and streams. Maybe even the plants."

Tom's stomach clenched as he thought of the possible implications behind Sam's words. "How?"

"It's caustic," Sam said simply. "In a high enough concentration, or with chronic exposure, we could see large fish die-offs, as well as a cascading effect through the plants and food chain."

Tom closed his eyes against yet another obstacle he felt helpless to fight against. Forcing himself to look again at the retreating storm, he thought of home and the vast plains, lakes, and streams that made Mercy a safe haven.

They had no idea what was coming for them.

CHAPTER 16

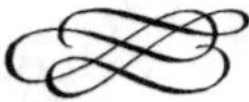

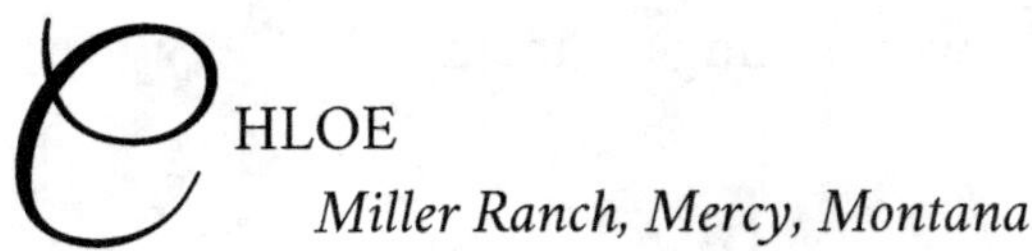

*C*HLOE
Miller Ranch, Mercy, Montana

THE WIND SHIFTED, carrying with it the scent of dry pine needles and fresh hay. Chloe pushed her bangs out of her face and straightened from the hay she was bucking, turning into the breeze and closing her eyes.

The silence was something Chloe welcomed. Her life had always been full of too much noise. Her first jog that morning had gone well and she already felt better. Like a small amount of the weight that was trying to smother her had lifted.

Chloe missed her exercise app, which would have told her exactly how far she went, but she guessed it was around five miles. Well, maybe four miles of running and another of walking. She wasn't in the best shape of her life.

Opening her eyes, Chloe stretched her back and looked at the last of the hay that still needed to be moved. She didn't pretend to get the whole system yet, though Sandy was doing her best to explain it. With the amount of cattle on the ranch, they were constantly rotating them through various fields, and also supplementing with hay. It was a continuous effort simply to keep the cows where they belonged and she understood now what Patty meant. They needed more people. It was that simple. The four of them might be able to keep up with the very basics of caring for the cattle, but it meant that almost every other aspect of the farm was suffering.

Chloe always did a lot of thinking when she jogged, and that morning she brainstormed about the farm's water problem and the woodstove conversion. Once the spring and farmer's market were both running more smoothly, they could borrow the muscle they needed to begin on their water issue. However, when it came to the stove, if Chloe had her way, they'd apply her latest ideas to the work-in-progress after dinner, and she'd be baking a pie before midnight. Or rather, Crissy and Sandy would. She was embarrassed to admit she didn't know how to make a pie.

"Earth to Chloe!" Crissy called out in a sing-song voice.

Chloe dropped her pitchfork and stared at her friend in surprise. She was working at the far end of one of the nearest fields, but it was still a good walk from the house. Crissy was picking her way through the tall grass and wiping her hands on one of Sandy's smocks she'd starting wearing when working with the chickens. Her long blonde hair was arranged in practical braids and she was makeup free. She looked healthy, and Chloe noticed with some suspicion that she had a curious spring in her step that bordered on happiness.

"I've got at least another hour of work out here," Chloe said before Crissy could get a word in. "If you're done with the chickens and gardening, you should grab a pitchfork!"

Crissy snorted. "Yeah, sure. Like I'll *ever* be done with the endless supply of weeds in that jungle Sandy calls a garden. This

—" she said while grabbing the tool out of Chloe's hands, "is called taking a break, Chlo. You know…where you sit down and do something silly, like talk with your best friend?" She unslung a bag from her shoulder, and pulled out a water bottle and piece of jerky. "I swear, I've hardly seen you in the past three days! You're out here before I even get up, and it seems like one of us is always asleep when the other one goes to bed."

Crissy was right, except she was exaggerating about their being separated. They'd just sat together at the barbeque the night before. Although, Chloe couldn't remember saying more than a few words to each other over the meal. She hadn't been in the best of moods. Feeling somewhat guilty, she took the offered snack and smiled at Crissy. "Thanks. And you're right, we need to make sure we do something together every once in a while besides work, eat, and sleep."

Crissy's smile widened. "I was hoping you'd say that."

"Uh-oh." Chloe had the distinct feeling she'd just been set up.

"Next week, on the Fourth of July, Tim is having a barn dance." Crissy clasped her hands together and stared excitedly at Chloe.

"Tim?"

Crissy rolled her eyes. "Tim. Tall, lanky, always wears that ridiculous straw-colored cowboy hat?"

"The guy that threw up when he had to help clean out Miss Hannigan's toilet?" Chloe raised an eyebrow, frowning at the thought of a barn full of dystopia-laden teens.

"That's the one," Crissy giggled. "But we don't talk about that day. Ever."

Laughing, Chloe chewed on the tasty jerky while trying to come up with a good enough excuse to bow out of the dance.

"You're not getting out of it," Crissy said, reading her mind. "It's already settled. Apparently, it's what passes around here for a party. A literal barn dance. I thought that was only something people sang about in country songs. Except that Tim's parents will be there, so there isn't going to be any alcohol, and only live music." Crissy stared off into space for a moment and then shook her head. "It doesn't matter! It's an excuse to take a bath, put on what passes for clean clothes, and have some fun!"

Maybe Crissy was right. While it felt almost disrespectful to have a party, at the same time, they were still kids. They were still alive, and they needed to find a way to move forward. If playing some bad banjo music in a barn for a few hours helped, then who was she to judge?

Chloe took a swig of water and then held the bottle out to Crissy with a smile. "Sounds like fun."

"Really?" Crissy sounded suspicious. "Because I thought I was going to have to learn how to hogtie you and throw you over a horse or something."

"I'm not *that* boring!" Chloe laughed. Or was she? She'd never actually been to a school dance. The thought reminded her that she didn't really know how to dance. Not that she planned on doing it at the barn, but what if someone asked her? That led to her worrying about what she'd wear. Sighing, Chloe grabbed the pitchfork and took a vicious stab at the hay bale. It was much easier to just work at the farm.

Sandy came into view in the distance, driving several cows ahead of her. Chloe was always impressed with the physical strength that the fifty-six-year-old woman displayed. Though not much taller than average, she was solidly built and could probably hold her own against most men. She sat tall and proud in the saddle, her black hair loose and trailing behind her, flowing out from under her cowboy hat.

"Where'd she come from?" Crissy asked, stepping up next to Chloe.

"Had to go find some cows that wandered off," Chloe explained, and then pointed to the south. "She's pretty worried about that weird storm that's been building up. Says it's got the animals all spooked."

Crissy raised a hand to her forehead to shield her eyes from the lowering sun and stared at the immense wall of clouds at the edge of the valley. "Are you sure it's even coming this way? I swear it's been swirling down there for more than a day."

Chloe hefted the last chunk of hay and walked with it to the feeder. Several cows had already lumbered over and more were on their way. "Sandy was sure of it this morning, and I think she's right. It definitely looks closer now. Come on." Chloe hooked an arm through Crissy's and started walking. "Come with me to the barn. If you help me muck the stalls, we'll have time for a game of gin rummy before we start dinner."

Crissy wrinkled her nose but didn't resist. "Only if you go with me after dinner to help collect eggs."

"Deal." Chloe knew it wasn't exactly a fair trade, but since it gave Crissy more of her desired "friend time", then she figured it wasn't really taking advantage of her.

As they approached the barn, they could hear Bishop hammering on something inside. Chloe thought he'd still be fishing and was surprised to find him bending over what looked like a giant wheel, propped up on sawhorses.

"Did you go fishing?" Chloe asked when he paused and looked up. There was an edge to her voice and he frowned at her. She might be totally sick of fish, but it was currently still one of their main sources of protein and what they'd planning to have for dinner.

Bishop waved wordlessly to a five-gallon bucket near the entrance. Chloe walked back to look inside and saw that there were four nice-looking trout. "Sorry," she offered, going back to stand next to him. "What are you working on?"

Pausing for a moment to give her one of his infamous "Bishop looks" to let her know he was going to let her rudeness pass while still acknowledging it. He then gestured to the wheel. "It's what it looks like. We desperately need another wagon. Not only for here on the farm, but for use around town. I studied the other one thoroughly, and I think that with some help from the local tradesmen, we should be able to make one. Maybe several, eventually."

Chloe was impressed. It was a brilliant idea. Without the ability to get any of the cars or tractors working in the near future, not to mention the whole gas-supply issue, the wagon was their best option. Especially with the amount of snow she was told they would get there in the winter. They'd need something tall enough to be able to plow through several feet of snow.

Bishop set his oversized hammer aside and lifted the wheel before setting it upright. Rolling it back and forth to check how even it was, he smiled in satisfaction. Crissy wasn't the only one who seemed to be benefiting from the farm life. Bishop looked comfortable in his role as a handyman and the large man seemed content wielding heavy tools and living off the land.

"Bishop, I'm glad you're here," Sandy called from the other end of the barn. She was still on her horse and Chloe thought she looked anxious. "I got those blasted cows back, but I need your help securing the upper pasture. That storm is coming fast now. I've never seen anything like it, and I don't want to have to go chasing after hundreds of cattle in its wake."

Bishop set the wheel back down without a word and started for his horse, which was still saddled and ready to go back out.

"Can we help?" Chloe offered.

"No," Sandy replied. "The two of us can handle it. Go ahead and work on dinner. We'll be back in a couple of hours."

As Bishop got on his horse and lifted a hand in a parting gesture, the sound of a galloping horse approaching made him pause. Chloe spun around to see a huge man riding up, and recognized him as Bishop's friend, Tane Latu.

"Bishop!" Tane shouted as he reached the barn. "I've been trying to call you on the handheld, but we think the storm is interfering with it."

"What's going on?" Sandy asked, having turned back. "What happened?"

Tane glanced at Crissy, and Chloe's stomach clenched.

"There was an accident this afternoon with the wagon." Tane shifted in his saddle and his mouth formed a grim line. "Three people died, Bishop, including Ned Allen."

Chloe struggled to remember who Ned Allen was, as Crissy leaned in close to her and whispered, "I think he was the old mayor of Mercy."

Sandy brought her horse farther into the barn, obviously upset by the news. "That's horrible, Tane! Is someone with his wife?"

Tane nodded and looked at Crissy again. "We also had a couple of others injured."

Crissy grasped Chloe's hand and they braced themselves.

"Your friend Trevor was seriously hurt, girls," Tane finally said. "I need you to come with me. He's asking for you."

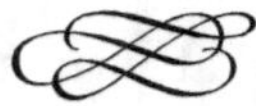

CHAPTER 17

PATTY
City Hall, Mercy, Montana

PATTY STARED at the faces surrounding her at the large table, tired of being in the same position yet again. It would never get any easier.

Caleb reached out and enveloped her hand with his, stopping their movement. Patty looked down at the contrast of his dark skin against hers and blinked a few times to clear her head. She hadn't even realized she was rubbing them together, almost frantically. She knew she was suffering from some post-traumatic stress. Even as a seasoned, albeit retired nurse, there were still some things that she'd see when she closed her eyes at night.

Patty resisted the urge to throw Caleb's hands off and check under her nails for blood. Ned Allen's blood. She took a shuddering breath. Once she allowed herself to cry, later that night while safe at home, she would be okay. She just had to keep it together for a couple more hours.

Closing her eyes, Patty didn't care that everyone was waiting for her to speak, to open the meeting. Just that morning, she'd still been holding out some hope that Ned would step back in as the mayor. Patty hadn't realized just how much she'd been relying on the older man's guidance and wisdom. What would she do without him?

Someone cleared their throat. Several people shifted in their chairs, and a man coughed. Patty turned and looked at Caleb for a moment, steeling herself for what had to be done. "We lost three good people today," she finally said, addressing the group. "Mr. and Mrs. Ferguson, who volunteered to transport the water, and…Councilman Ned Allen."

There were a couple of gasps and Betty, their other councilwoman, sobbed openly. Patty didn't know if it was because they somehow hadn't heard the news yet, or if perhaps having it said out loud made it more real and inescapable. She wished Bishop and Sandy were there. Although they'd recently had their disagreements, they were both people the other town leaders looked up to. Patty of all people understood that securing the herd ahead of the storm was more important than a meeting, but the extra support would have been nice.

"From what we could tell at the accident scene, and based on Trevor's account of what happened, it's likely the water container shifted when they hit a pothole," Sheriff Waters explained. "It was the steepest part of the gravel road and they were going too fast. That old wagon simply wasn't able to handle it. The right wheel broke off and the whole thing rolled over the edge of the road."

Patty shuddered, recalling the grisly scene. When she and Caleb arrived with Melissa, several people were trying to pull the five-hundred-gallon water tank off their bodies using ropes and horses. It was positioned so that they couldn't easily release the water from it.

Bishop had done the math early on in their venture to transport the spring water, so Patty knew the container weighed over four thousand pounds. The Fergusons had been instantly crushed to death. Ned Allen hadn't been so lucky. They managed to get his mangled body back to the clinic, where Patty sat with him for over an hour while he died. Melissa tried to keep on top of his pain with morphine, but…Patty shook her head, realizing she was rubbing her hands together again.

"That wagon should have never been used to transport so much weight in the first place," Gary interjected.

"According to the history books, those wagons were designed to haul up to six tons of freight," Fire Chief Martinez yelled at Gary. "I did the research myself. The water wasn't more than two tons!"

"It was almost two hundred years old!" Gary countered. "Is it even salvageable?"

Melissa's head jerked at the comment and she glared at Gary. "Seriously, Gary?" the doctor gasped. "Three people are dead, and your main concern is the wagon?"

Gary at least had the decency to appear chastised, though he didn't look away from Melissa. "I don't mean to sound callous, but we're in a lot of trouble without our main means of transportation. Someone here needs to be thinking about that," he had the nerve to add while staring pointedly at Patty.

"He's right," Patty said before anyone else could get involved. Caleb raised his eyebrows at her in surprise. "This tragedy needs to serve as yet another reminder of the constant, precarious situation we're in," she said with emotion. "We've already started building two new wagons, and if it continues to go well, the first one should be ready in a day or two."

"We're going to salvage some of the parts from the old one to speed the process up," Sheriff Waters added. "Manufacturing those more specific pieces was going to be the greatest challenge to—"

"When are the funerals?" Betty interrupted. Everyone turned to look at the young schoolteacher. "I understand how important the wagon is. I just think Ned deserves more respect. And the Fergusons. Their daughter was in my class. So...*when* is the funeral?" she asked again, turning that time to look at the new pastor, Father Rogers, who quietly leaned against the back wall.

Patty groaned inwardly. She'd forgotten that in the midst of everything that had happened, while leaving the clinic she'd invited both of the priests to the impromptu meeting. Her intent had been to acknowledge their help and introduce Father Russell Rogers. Father White declined the invitation, saying he was too tired and wasn't feeling well.

"Father White will be meeting with the remaining family members or close friends tomorrow, to discuss plans for a service and burial," Russell explained, his voice smooth and calming. He subtly pushed away from the wall and took a step closer to Betty. "I apologize that I don't know who the deceased's relatives are, but I can assure you Father White will handle it all respectfully."

Betty appeared placated and Patty silently thanked Russell for his intervention. He certainly had a way with people. "I'm sorry for not introducing Father Rogers sooner," Patty said, gesturing to the handsome man. "I'm sure you've all heard about his arrival by now and that he's come to us all the way from Wyoming. He's already been a great help and is staying in the church apartment."

Patty leaned back in her seat and welcomed the reprieve the few minutes of introductions gave her. Russell worked his way around the table, taking time to meet each person and exchange some sort of pleasantry. All of them responded positively; a couple even laughed at whatever he said.

"Excuse me?" Mr. Sullivan, the old storekeeper stood and raised a hand in the air while speaking.

"Go ahead," Patty encouraged. Mr. Sullivan never spoke much

at the meetings. Although there wasn't much left in his store, he still had a vast knowledge from his many years of living in Mercy.

"We're…um, we seem to be all out of toilet paper." He sat back down amid some chuckles and open laughter from around the room.

"This is actually a very legitimate concern," Fire Chief Martinez said. "If people start putting things in their septic systems that aren't compatible, no one's going to be laughing about it."

The laughter died down as everyone contemplated one of the simplest things they'd taken for granted throughout their lives. Toilet paper. Patty put a hand to her forehead. She simply didn't have the resolve to think about anything else that night. Not even the demise of their septics and raw backsides.

"If you'd like, I can talk with a couple of the ladies who are supplying me with their homemade soaps and other products," Mr. Sullivan offered. "They might have some ideas."

"Thank you, Mr. Sullivan," Patty said with sincerity. "Since this isn't one of our normal meetings, I didn't bring any of the binders with me. I'll come by tomorrow or the next day with a new one for you and we can come up with some more plans. Okay?"

Mr. Sullivan nodded, satisfied with the plan, and Patty turned her focus back to the rest of the weary group. "I think that's more than enough for now. I'm not sure about the rest of you, but I know Caleb and I would really like to get home before that storm lets loose on us."

There were several mumbles of agreement, but Melissa stood before Patty could officially close the meeting. "One more thing," she called out above the din. "Trevor, the young man who has been helping me so diligently at the clinic, was also hurt in the wagon accident. He's going to be okay, but will be off his feet for some time. With only one nurse and two other volunteers helping me, I'm going to be struggling again to get around and check on everyone."

"I'd be happy to help you," Father Rogers said without any hesitation.

Melissa turned to face the priest, her eyebrows raised. "Are you sure, Father? It's a lot of long hours full of very tedious work."

Father Rogers shrugged his shoulders and smiled at Melissa, and Patty was again struck by how handsome the man was. She could only imagine how captivating his sermons would be. "Honestly, I have nothing else to do right now and I do have some medical background. Not a lot, but probably enough to at least be more help than hinderance."

Melissa smiled back and Patty was almost certain she was blushing. "That would be great, Father. If you can come by in the morning after you get some breakfast, I could use some help right away."

Russell nodded and then moved his gaze to Patty. "Thank you for welcoming me into Mercy, Mayor Woods. I only hope I can return the kindness."

"You already have," Patty answered, glad that he had found a way to fit in, in spite of Father White's continued aversion to him. While the older priest hadn't said anything more to her in the past day, it was quite obvious when he was working with him earlier at the clinic that they weren't getting along very well.

"Let's meet again in a few days to discuss the wagons, the next town barbeque, which also happens to be the Fourth of July, and all of the other normal updates," Patty concluded as everyone began to rise. Backing away from the table, she started rubbing her hands together again as she walked over to the whiteboard still sitting at the back of the room. It was blank, except for the number 640 written in the middle. The green ink was in her own handwriting, but Patty could hardly remember drawing it. Taking a deep breath, she rubbed away the four and zero with the edge of her left hand while picking up the same green pen with her right. Slowly, almost reverently, she wrote the new population of 638. Would there ever come a day when the numbers increased instead of dwindled?

Her heart heavy, Patty went to set the pen back down, but paused as a surreal sound tore through the air. Spinning back towards the windows, Patty saw that everyone in the room had frozen in fear as the screeching reached a crescendo. Betty covered her ears, Mr. Sullivan ducked down behind the table and Caleb was reaching out to her. Patty struggled to understand what was happening…it was as if a train was about to hit the building, its brakes wailing in protest, while at the same time a cheetah roared and a waterfall gushed.

Then, something *did* hit the building, only it wasn't a train, but a wall of water and howling wind. The storm was there, and as everyone gasped with the realization, Patty was terrified that her words from only minutes earlier would prove to be prophetic. Once again, they were unprepared and this time there was no telling what the damage would be.

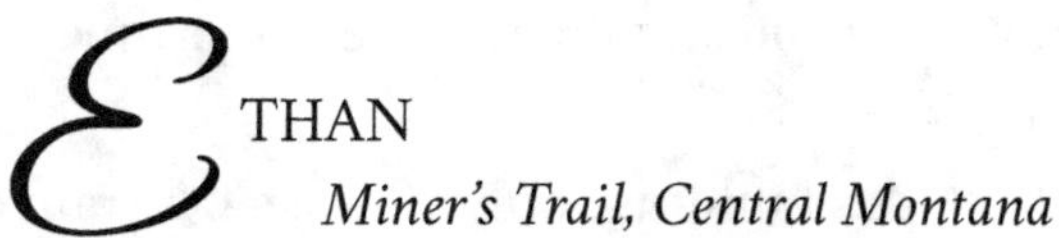

$\mathcal{E}$THAN
Miner's Trail, Central Montana

"I WANT you to ride Lily the rest of the way." Tom stared down at Ethan with his arms crossed over his chest and it was obvious he wasn't in the mood to debate the situation.

However, his dad's moodiness never stopped Ethan before. "I'm fine!" he argued, taking another bite of his biscuit. Anna had packed enough of the hard rolls and huckleberries to feed them for a couple of days. Sam was already putting dirt on the fire and Danny was tying down the last of the bags on the pack horse. Sighing audibly, Ethan got slowly to his feet, displacing Grace from his lap. She glanced up at him with a hurt look and so he held out the last of his bread to her.

"Are you?" Tom asked, his eyebrows raised. "Go ahead and lift your pack then. With only your right arm!" he added, when Ethan took hold of a strap in either hand.

Grunting, Ethan attempted to do as his father demanded, and

could only lift it half of the way. His face pinched with pain; he dropped the bag back on the ground unceremoniously. "So I can't lift my stupid backpack. That doesn't mean I can't sit on a horse." Ethan knew he was whining and he glanced over at Danny, who wasn't trying to hide the fact that she was listening. Sam at least had the decency to pretend to be doing something else.

"It's not about sitting on a horse, and you know it." Tom retorted. "You haven't been on the length of that trail, Ethan. There's a very steep, rocky section that I wouldn't want you to take Tango through, even with a good arm. He's too flighty and we've never had him on a trail like that. It's a chance I'm not willing to take, so I'll be riding him instead."

"I have to agree with your dad," Danny added, moving closer. Ethan turned his pained expression on her and she smiled at his antics. "Your arm is probably only bruised, maybe sprained, but without any real way to examine it we don't know for sure that you didn't break something. A hard yank on the reins and certainly a fall on a steep, rocky trail isn't something you need to risk."

Ethan expected his dad to be irritated at the interruption, but instead, he gave Danny a thankful grin. "What?" Ethan said, stopping Sam as he attempted to walk by with another handful of dirt he didn't need. "You aren't going to get in on this?"

"I figure you have enough sense to work this out on your own." Winking, Sam tossed the dirt and then whistled for Grace. "Time to get going."

Sam understood how Ethan's brain worked way too well. Ethan knew his dad was right. If he were honest about it, he would admit to having a hard time keeping the gelding in check for the rest of their ride the night before, and that was on a relatively flat surface.

It had turned out to be another ten miles to the campground, where the trail met up with State Route 12 for a short distance. There had been too many people there for any of their comfort, so they had continued down the road for another few miles until his dad found the other trailhead.

Ethan understood why his dad wanted to find it before dark. He was just as eager to be on that final stretch, but it made for a really long day and he was still tired and very sore. Another night sleeping on the cold ground had emphasized all the new bruises he got from being hit by the tree.

"Fine," Ethan huffed, picking the pack back up with his left arm. "But I'm pretty sure there's got to be some sort of cowboy code about never taking a man's horse away."

Tom stared at him for moment before laughing out loud. He surprised Ethan by reaching out and ruffling his hair in a playful manner, the way he always used to. When was the last time he'd done that? Probably not since the first day of the flashpoint. Maybe even longer. The totally normal gesture brought on such a surge of unexpected emotions that Ethan had to turn away. He knew his dad probably took it the wrong way, but he wasn't about to have a breakdown in front of everyone.

Walking to Lily without daring to look back, Ethan patted wordlessly at his thigh for Grace. The retriever responded immediately and he felt better as soon as her cold nose nudged against his hand. Kneeling down, he pretended to simply pet her back and tell her to follow him, when he was in fact using her calming presence to help him control his racing heart.

Ethan had begun to experience what he thought were panic attacks. His mom struggled with it and even took medication periodically. He'd never understood why she couldn't simply shake it off, or whatever. Yeah...it wasn't that easy.

His breathing back under control again, Ethan found further comfort in the familiar motions of mounting the horse. He was thankful that the sun was shining so they wouldn't have to suffer through another miserable, wet, cold day. In fact, the sky was the darkest blue it had been in over a week and for the first time since they started the whole journey, he couldn't smell the smoke from burning cities. It had a distinctly acrid scent to it. While the storm had been terrifying, it also turned out to be cleansing. Plus, they were heading due north and steadily climbing higher into the mountains. Montana was called Big Sky Country for good reason.

"Hopefully we won't have a bunch of trees to get around," Sam said as they all fell into line. Unlike the section they'd been on when the storm hit, now the trail was narrower and surrounded by dense forest. Although the debris from the storm wasn't as bad, there were still plenty of branches and an occasional uprooted tree trunk.

"The worst part of the trail is on a rocky ledge," Tom said. "There aren't many trees through there so it shouldn't be a problem."

"Why doesn't that make me feel better?" Danny said sarcastically.

"You'll be fine," Tom reassured her. "Just give the horse her head and hold on. If it's too bad, you can always get off and walk."

Based on Danny's expression, Ethan figured she'd be doing her fair share of hiking over the next two days. Two days…he smiled. Could they really be that close to finally being home at the ranch? The thought of sleeping in his own room and bed was enough to dispel the last of his anxiousness.

With Tom leading the way, they set a good pace and there wasn't much talking for the first couple of hours. Grace would bark and chase after the occasional squirrel, but otherwise, they were surrounded by a pristine, raw landscape and profound silence.

As they traveled above what had to be more than five thousand feet, the trees thinned out and deer trails began to intersect with their own narrowing one, making it harder to define which was which.

"Be sure to keep an eye out for any herds," Tom called back to Ethan as the sun rose higher and continued to dry out the foliage.

"Do you mean deer?" Danny asked.

Ethan twisted around in his saddle and rolled his eyes at her. "Why in the world would we look for deer when we can hunt elk?"

"Sorry," Danny said, making a face back at him good-humoredly. "I'm not a hunter. I know how to shoot…I'm actually pretty good at it, but I've never shot an animal."

"Please don't tell me you're one of those people who don't believe in it," Tom said, sounding genuinely concerned.

Danny snorted. "Of course not! Even if I were, I think our current situation would trump any of my aversions to animal cruelty. We need to eat. If you teach me how, I'd be happy to bring Bambi…er, I mean, whatever you'd call an elk home for dinner."

"I don't think I've ever eaten elk," Sam said, from the back of the line. "I've heard it can be kind of gamey."

"Depends," Ethan said, enjoying the conversation. "If an elk is butchered and cooked right, it doesn't taste gamey. It has a stronger flavor than beef, but I think it's good."

"We can also hunt for duck later this year, and black bears," Tom added. "I've never gotten into tanning, but it might be something we should consider learning."

Ethan frowned at that troubling observation. "You mean for our clothes and stuff?" He had a sudden, daunting image of them dressed in fur leggings and ponchos.

Tom chuckled and glanced over his shoulder at him. "I'm pretty sure we'll be able to salvage plenty of other things for clothes before we resort to using hides. I was thinking more for rugs and leather. It's going to be cold this winter, with only a fireplace to keep us warm. Some bear rugs on the floor would be nice. And you'd be amazed at how many uses you can come up with for leather."

Ethan mulled it all over for a while. He wasn't sure what he thought about it. The idea of living off the land had always been something he thought he'd enjoy. Now that he faced it and all of the different aspects of what it really meant, he wasn't so sure it seemed as appealing.

Thinking about the luxuries of his previous lifestyle in the fancy home in Vegas made Ethan remember his mom. It wasn't that he'd really forgotten about her, he just didn't allow himself to think about her. It was too hard. Shifting in the saddle, Ethan tried to focus instead on the surrounding countryside, and any signs of elk. But his mom's image kept creeping back into his thoughts. The details were already getting fuzzy. How could he not remember which cheek her mole was on? Or to which side she usually wore her bangs? The knowledge that his photo album waited safely tucked away at the bottom of his bag was the only thing that kept him from giving in again to the vise that was trying to tighten around his chest. He did have a picture. It was a few years old, but she really hadn't changed much since it was taken. They'd been on a trip to the beach, a condo in Malibu his stepdad rented for a weekend. One of his many attempts to "bond" with Ethan.

If he closed his eyes, he could almost feel the constant breeze on the beach, smell the salty air, and hear the gulls crying. He could hear his mother's light, musical laughter, and the way she would always tell him that she loved him. The greatest love of her life, she would say, while holding him tight against her chest.

Lily took an extra step to clear a decent-sized log and Ethan was jerked back to the present. It was one full of unknowns and things that could be seen as either obstacles or opportunities. He supposed it was all in the way you looked at it.

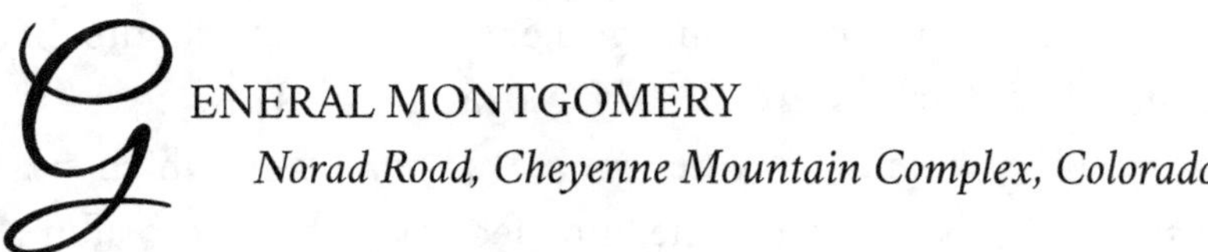

CHAPTER 19

GENERAL MONTGOMERY
Norad Road, Cheyenne Mountain Complex, Colorado

GENERAL ANDREW MONTGOMERY stared out at the somewhat arid landscape of the Colorado Springs suburb. An impressive neighborhood of nice homes backed up against the base's boundary. At least, it used to be impressive, before a third of it was ravaged by fire. The rest was now rapidly becoming overgrown and strewn with garbage and tents. He had a nice view of it all from his perch, partway up the mountain.

"I didn't expect to find you this far up the road." Colonel Walsh's head appeared above the edge of the boulder he was sitting on.

Hanging his head, the general sighed and threw his hands up in the air. "And yet, find me you did." He brushed some dirt from the stone next to him and then patted it. "Come on, have a seat. It's really a lovely day."

Walsh hesitated, appearing uncertain if his commander was being serious or not. When Montgomery continued to simply stare out over the valley, he scrambled the rest of the way up the rock and took the offered spot. "Your color is looking a little better."

"The doctor insisted I come topside to get my vitamin D," Montgomery said flatly. Tipping his face up towards the sun, he winced as if it were burning. "I take orders seriously. So, here I am."

He saw Walsh frown, knowing that the younger man figured the comment was meant as a dig for some infraction he'd unknowingly committed. It wasn't, of course. Walsh's commitment to detail was admirable, though he never wanted his assistant to get too comfortable.

"The city is still burning," he observed, leaving Walsh to guess what it was he might have done. "How long do you think it'll last?"

"There's a lot of fuel. It could smolder for weeks."

The general mulled that over for a moment. "And what's with the line of people at the gate? There are more than I thought there'd be by now."

"They're still mostly local residents," Walsh answered. He pointed at the first gated entry to the complex, which was located several miles down Norad Road and past several parking lots and guard shacks. "We give them some water and re-direct them to either one of the local civilian shelters, or else FEMA CO1. Most are satisfied and seem relieved to finally have someone to tell them what to do."

"And the altercation last night?" Montgomery stared into the sun again, intentionally avoiding eye contact with Walsh.

The colonel cleared his throat, a nervous gesture he'd developed over the years. "It was unfortunate, sir. Two armed men approached the gate and refused to identify themselves. They continued to demand entry and raised their weapons, forcing the guards to fire upon them. I left a full report on your desk."

"I read it." The general finally faced Walsh, his profile dark in the afterglow from the sun. "As I'm sure Vice Admiral Baker did, too."

"So, you've heard of the rumors coming out of Albuquerque."

"The admiral is doing a solid job of making sure everyone of importance hears those stories," Montgomery growled, his sunshine-infused happiness rapidly fading. "He's well aware the clinic was attacked by the group that had taken over the FEMA shelter, not our men. However, it would seem those details are getting left out."

General Montgomery forced himself to take a breath of the fresh air, although slightly tinged with smoke, and got his emotions in check. He couldn't let Vice Admiral Baker get to him. Instead, he focused on Walsh and why he'd sought him out. "Are you going to tell me why you're sitting on the side of this mountain with me? Because I know it isn't to discuss water-lines and rumors."

"Governor Alicia Jenson," Walsh said without any further preamble.

Montgomery frowned, trying to place the name. "The governor out of Idaho?"

"That's the one," Walsh confirmed.

"Why would I care about the governor of Idaho?"

Walsh cleared his throat again. "Because she's invoking her right to appoint herself as the new senator for her state, and is calling upon the other remaining governors to do the same."

It didn't take Montgomery long to put it together. His eyes widened and his nostrils flared. "If she can manage to get a quorum together, they can vote for a president pro tempore." In the civilian government, the head of the senate, or the president pro tempore, was the third in succession for the presidency, after the Speaker of the House. If she succeeded in the gambit, they could legally appoint a new president.

General Montgomery had the utmost respect for their former administration. However, it was clear that the current attempt to usurp the military and their declaration of martial law was not in the best interest of the people.

Walsh wisely remained silent as the general thought about the possible scenarios. "Break down the numbers for me," Montgomery demanded after a few minutes. His voice was curt and he'd lost any of his previous goodwill.

"Out of the nineteen viable states, we've had confirmed contacts with eleven of the governors, though one of those is Hawaii, so we won't count her for now." Walsh shifted uncomfortably on the hard rock, but his face remained neutral. "One of the senators for California was home on vacation during the flashpoint, so he's the most likely candidate for the president pro tempore."

Montgomery waved a hand dismissively. "I don't care about who they are right now. I'll leave it to you to worry about the politics and fill me in if it becomes necessary. For now, I want to know the logistics and the feasibility of them pulling this off."

"Governor Jenson is trying to organize a meeting in southern Idaho for later next month." Walsh hesitated, and the general lost his patience.

"If you have something more to tell me, then get on with it!" Montgomery stood slowly and looked down at the colonel. When he still failed to speak or even look up at him, he squatted next to Walsh, his uniform protesting the movement. "What is it, Kelly?"

Walsh stared out at the suburbs of Colorado Springs and gave his head a shake in disgust. "One of my men intercepted a message from Admiral Baker earlier this morning. He's assisting Governor Jenson in her efforts, Sir."

Montgomery wished he could say he was surprised, except that the news was almost expected. Actually, it would work out perfectly with his other...plans. A small smile played at the corners of his lips so he turned away from Walsh and walked across the top of the rock with his hands clasped behind his back. "Do you have any other morsels of information for me, Colonel?"

Walsh rose slowly and stood staring at the general's back. "Just that reports of militia activity is increasing. It still isn't anything that's truly organized, but enough for Jenson and Baker to use to their advantage when carrying on about crimes against humanity."

Montgomery turned his head to look back over his left shoulder. "Explain."

"Governor Jenson's 'platform', for lack of a better word, is that our mishandling of the military response is forcing civilians to take up arms to protect themselves."

Montgomery snorted. "That's ridiculous, and anyone with common sense will see that. But..." he paced the length of the rock again, his eyes narrowed in concentration. "Why make it easy for them?"

"Sir?" Walsh sounded wary.

"Calling these random bands of thugs militia is giving them too much credit," Montgomery said thoughtfully. "Ignoring them isn't an option, of course, but from now on, let's call them what they really are. Terrorists. Begin daily bulletins, to be distributed and communicated to all active states, highlighting their crimes."

Walsh pursed his lips and then nodded. "We start an aggressive campaign now, labeling them as terrorists and claiming their responsibility for the attacks being blamed on our men."

General Montgomery knew he could count on his friend to rapidly connect the dots. "As militia, we're allowing the admiral and Governor Jenson to use them as an excuse to bring the people together to fight against a blood-thirsty dictatorship.

However, if they're the ones using terrorists to push their cause, I would say that makes them a tyrant and a traitor, instead of revolutionaries. Wouldn't you agree, Colonel?"

Walsh appeared uncomfortable again, though he held his tongue.

"When is the first convoy from Mount Weather due to arrive in Denver?" Montgomery asked, already working his new angle.

"Not until next week," Walsh answered. "The logistics have proven incredibly difficult, but they're still making reasonable progress."

"Have one of the large caches delivered to Peterson as soon as possible." Montgomery turned to look to where the Air Force base was located on the far side of Colorado Springs.

"Sir?"

"Don't sound so surprised, Colonel," Montgomery chastised. "Assign no fewer than a dozen soldiers to work with the local civilian shelters to get them what they need. And have all of that garbage down there cleaned up. Dig a pit or something for it before the smell spreads. We can use Colorado Springs as an example of what we can accomplish once the dust has settled and we get the supplies dispersed. I want a detailed plan on how to get this city back under control."

"Yes, sir. I already have a contact list for the local government. We've been able to locate a handful of them."

Montgomery rubbed at his jaw as he considered the intel. "A committee."

"A civilian committee?" Walsh pressed.

"Don't politicians love committees?" The general smiled then as his idea continued to form. "I want you to personally approach the highest remaining civilian official in Colorado Springs, and request that he head a committee to work with us on how to rebuild their town."

"That would be the mayor. You know, Mr. Fine?" Walsh

frowned. "He's made several attempts to speak with you since the flashpoint, sir."

"Then he should be thrilled by this news," Montgomery snapped. He had hoped to avoid any politics for a few more months, but he should have known it wouldn't be possible. Even with martial law declared and the literal fate of the world hanging in the balance, there would be those of influence trying to jockey for a position of power. It was all a matter of smoke and mirrors, and knowing when and how to make a move. Fortunately, while the general despised politics, he was a master chess player.

"There was one more reason I came to find you," Walsh said while looking back down the road, obviously eager to leave.

"I'm assuming it's in regards to my new orders for Vice Admiral Baker?" Montgomery had expected it to be an issue.

"I've got them written up and am ready to deliver it, but…"

"I imagine he'll make a scene," Montgomery finished for the other man. "Yes, yes. I'm well aware of that, and how in light of these other recent events it might be seen as a form of retaliation. But you know what, Colonel?"

Colonel Walsh knew it was a rhetorical question, and kept his mouth shut.

"One of the benefits of being in command means I don't always have to answer to someone," the general said, his face more animated than usual. "If anyone wants to challenge my decision, they can write a formal complaint and I'll be sure to give it my utmost attention."

"He might refuse." Walsh stood then and approached the general. "He could use this against you."

"You make it sound as if this traitor has a backbone," Montgomery spat. "I've known Baker for years and while he's a big talker, if you remove his support, he'll wither right before your eyes. Besides, I'm simply giving the man what he's been demanding for the past two weeks. He wants us to actively get out there and intervene with the actions of these terrorists. So be it."

"But a field assignment?" Walsh pushed. "It's unheard of to have a vice admiral getting his boots muddy."

"These are unusual times." Montgomery jumped the few feet down from the rock and made his way to the gravel road he'd hiked up to reach it. Looking back, he waited for Walsh to catch up. "Vice Admiral Baker is barely fifty, Colonel. And he's led men in the field for more years than most have even been in the military. If he's so eager to cause dissent, then he can at least make some use of himself while he's doing it."

Walsh moved up alongside him, looking resigned. "Yes, sir. I'll deliver the orders after lunch."

"Take an armed escort with you," Montgomery said as they began walking. He'd made another mistake by underestimating the threat the admiral posed. It was time to advance from the scrambling they'd been doing the past two weeks and focus more on the future.

It would, of course, be a travesty if the admiral were to find himself face-to-face with some of his "militia". General Montgomery stopped and squared his shoulders before barking out one final order. "Colonel, get that bastard out of my mountain."

CHAPTER 20

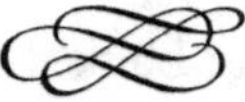

$\mathcal{J}$AMES
  Master Sergeant, US Marines, 1st Force Recon-
naissance
Butte, Montana

"So, who's the asset, Sarge?" Jay leaned in close to James so he wouldn't have to yell to be heard in the back of the helicopter.

James hadn't been totally honest with the general when he said the mission would be the same as any other. He would carry out the op—that wasn't an issue. It was the evasiveness toward the rest of his team that bothered him the most. 1st Force Recon was a family, in some ways even more so than a nuclear one. Keeping secrets from each other could end up getting them killed, so his orders didn't sit well with him. Clenching his jaw, he didn't meet his friend's eyes. "Just another scientist."

Jay sat back and stared at him until James finally turned his head to face him. "Come on, Terminator. We've known each other too long to pull this crap with each other."

130

Using his handle was going back to their old days together in basics. James wasn't sure why the information was so important to Jay. He didn't usually care about the details so long as he was clear about his role. It was likely because he could tell James was acting differently, which made him nervous.

Sitting up straight, he did the only thing he could do. Pull rank. "Do we have a problem, Gunnery Sergeant Terrill?"

Jay's face reddened and he glanced over at Lee and O'Grady, who were close enough to hear most of the exchange. "No, sir. I only thought it might help us avoid getting killed if we had a better idea this time of what we're walking into."

"My understanding is that we're making entry into a two-story wooden structure located in the middle of an upper middle-class suburb in Butte," Sergeant O'Grady rattled off.

"Shut up, Lucas," Jay barked, clearly not in the mood to joke around. "I'm more interested in the who and why, rather than the where."

"You know everything you need to," James said gruffly while leveling Jay with a look that made it clear the discussion was over. At some point, he'd be able to explain the whole mess to his best friend and get his valued input, but not yet. He was under strict orders and he was a soldier first, above all else.

"At least we learned something from our op in Albuquerque," Corporal Flores said with optimism, while pointing at a crate full of bottled water.

James smiled and then jerked his chin toward Jay. "It was a good idea, Sergeant."

"Just a simple slight of hand," Jay replied, still sullen.

Unlike the necessarily direct approach they had to make at the military base, the rural neighborhood offered several more options. The houses sat on lots from a quarter to a full acre in size, and had several greenbelts they would make good use of. It was currently around lunchtime, so they didn't have the advantage of an early morning or late-night operation, but they shouldn't need it.

The latest report coming out of the smaller town was that there was plenty of unrest and the usual anarchy and destruction. However, without any large targets of interest, such as a military base or FEMA shelter, it wasn't considered a hot zone. Easy pickings for a team of highly trained Marines.

Four of the men would INFIL at the nearest greenbelt, while Helo One then transported Alphas Five and Six to the opposite side of town. From there, they would draw any attention away from the insert team by dropping water and bags of peanuts. The rations had been Jay's idea, and it was a good one. It not only helped with their mission, but also allowed them to give some aid and leave a better impression. They were all aware of the rumors surrounding their last op. It didn't matter if they were true or not, just that people were saying it.

Five clicks.

The pilot's voice cut into his thoughts as it filtered through his headset and James made a wind-up motion with his hand. The other five men in the back of the helo moved almost in unison, like a well-choreographed dance. Donning the rest of their FSBE—full spectrum battle equipment—and TASC communication gear, they then quickly and methodically went through their final checks.

Amidst a flurry of hand signals, James moved aft to the open door and waited as they approached the INFIL point. If the maps proved accurate, there would be a field more than big enough to accommodate them near the greenbelt. Resting a hand on his M4, James studied the landscape slipping by as they swooped in. It was the same as any other city they'd seen. Fires still burned and groups of people milled about. He didn't see any sign of an organized, armed force, or large encampments that were obvious. As they slid over the tops of a row of houses, he recognized the neighborhood and had to take a second calming breath, before giving the order.

"Go, go, go," James spoke into his headset while also motioning to his team, and he was the first to leap from the helo as it hovered several feet above the grassy field. Landing in a crouch, he then moved forward cautiously, not taking anything about their situation for granted.

As the four soldiers ambled swiftly toward the belt of evergreens, James once again contemplated the viability of the op. The reality was if the asset didn't want to be found, he wouldn't be. His training was just as rigorous as the 1st Force Recon Unit… maybe more. The fact that he'd fallen off the radar after one soft contact spoke volumes to James. He didn't understand it, but trusted that the man had his reasons. Good ones.

Once under the cover of the trees, the men stood and ran at a swifter pace, covering the quarter mile in a matter of minutes. By the time they reached the far side that butted up against several wooden fence lines, marking private backyards, Helo One could be seen hovering above what must have been the far side of town.

"Alpha One to Helo One," James said, eying the bird.

Go for Helo One.

"Helo One, what's your SITREP?"

Helo One is over our target site. Ready to drop the package. Drawing some attention but no Tango contact.

"That's a hard copy, Helo One. Closing in on position two."

James moved up to the five-foot wooden fence and peered into the yard. He didn't recognize it, but the one next to it was familiar. Raising his right hand, James motioned to the house on their left and then crept the length of the fence to where it met with the other homes thick hedge.

Leaping over the lower barrier, the four soldiers jogged silently across the grass. A dog barked from somewhere up the block and a baby could be heard crying. A sudden scraping sound nearby caused James to spin and drop to a knee.

"Hey!" a man cried in alarm. He had just come out his patio door, dressed in dirty shorts and bare-chested. Aside from a bottle of beer, he was empty-handed and clearly not a threat. Throwing his hands up, he dropped the beer, and stared wide-eyed at the soldiers.

"Get back inside!" James ordered, eying the spilled beer. What a waste.

As the terrified neighbor did as he was told, James continued into the next yard. He wasn't too concerned about the unexpected contact, since short of running outside and yelling, there wasn't any way to communicate to anyone that he had seen them. Plus, there was a very real chance that the guy would be hiding in his closet for a while.

"Alpha One to Helo One," James spoke into his headset as he approached the sliding glass door of the target house.

Go for Helo One.

"We've reached position two. Making entry."

Helo One copies. Still no Tango contact. The natives are happily distributing the goods.

James tried the door. Confirming it was locked, he took a step back and nodded at Alpha Three. Moving forward, the other man made quick work of the lock and then stepped aside.

"Alphas Three and Four, you hold the perimeter," James directed. "Alpha Two, you're with me."

Jay exchanged a quick look with the other two men, but no one commented on the change in the approach. James was counting on his men's trust to carry them through the mission, and hopefully, to salvage their friendship afterward.

"Clear!" Jay called from the nearest room as James moved toward the front of the house. They would conduct a standard sweep pattern, but he already knew what the result would be.

There obviously wasn't anyone there and likely hadn't been since before the flashpoint. If the asset had made it back after the event, the house would have been fortified and they certainly wouldn't have gained entry so easily.

He heard Jay climbing the stairs to the second floor where there were two bedrooms and two baths. The bottom floor contained a guest room, family room, and office, in addition to the large country kitchen.

James traveled stoically through the space, going through the steps robotically and without emotion. Making quick work of it, he ended at the threshold to the office. A large wooden desk sat facing the French doors, an inviting bay window behind it. The two side walls were covered with built-in bookcases, and the floor had a thick accent rug with warm colors. The only other furniture was an overstuffed leather chair positioned near one of the walls. There was a small side table next to it with a darkened Tiffany lamp. When lit, it would have been inviting for someone to sit and read one of the hundreds of books. Now, it stood as a form of mockery. An expensive piece of artwork that might never shed light again.

Master Sergeant James Campbell stood with his hand on the frame of the doorway, one foot in the office. He knew how misleading the room was. That it portrayed a man of silent intelligence. Perhaps a college professor or some other literary powerhouse who wielded a pen instead of a sword. James knew the truth.

Moving with more resolve, he crossed to the desk. Filtered light from the bay window revealed that amongst several other items, there was a closed laptop and an empty notepad next to it. Pushing the desk chair aside, James crouched down and began sorting through the meaningless clutter until he found what he was looking for. Picking up the calendar, he grimaced when he saw the highlighted days for the week of the flashpoint. The asset was on vacation for several days prior to, and during the event.

Raising a finger to trace the hastily scribbled notes that riddled the paper, James didn't know if he was disappointed or relieved to know the asset wasn't there. Dropping the calendar onto the laptop, he picked them both up. The computer was likely fried, but the technicians at Cheyenne Mountain might be able to salvage something off the hard drive.

"Alpha One to Alpha Team, the asset has flown the coop. Move to EXFIL."

Before James could get around the desk, Sergeant Terrill walked into the office, looking unhappy. "Well, this was a freaking waste of time, Sarge."

"Maybe not," James answered, hefting the laptop. "We might be able to figure out where he is." As Jay advanced further into the room, James attempted to cut him off while gesturing back the way they'd come. "Let's get out of here."

It must have been too much, because his friend paused, and after staring questioningly at him, took a second look around the office. Casually running a hand along the nearest bookshelf, Jay accidentally knocked a couple of pictures onto the floor. Bending to pick them up, he happened to glance down at the image as he stood.

James snatched the photograph away from him, but he knew it was too late. "I said let's move out."

Jay put a hand up to stop him, and then pointed at the picture. "Not until you tell me what the hell is going on, James! Who is that man? What's your connection to the asset?"

James turned the frame over and stared at the image. It had been taken on their annual hunting trip two years earlier. "He's my dad."

CHAPTER 21

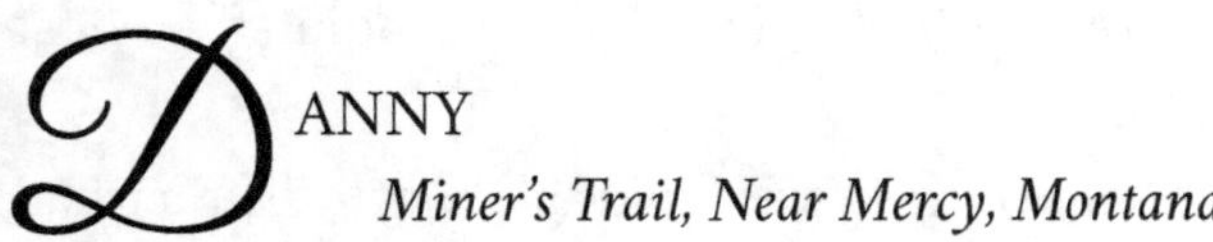

DANNY

Miner's Trail, Near Mercy, Montana

IF DANNY HADN'T BEEN SO terrified of falling off the side of the mountain, she would have enjoyed the incredible scenery more.

"I think we'd be better off riding mountain goats," Sam called out from his spot at the back of the line. Every time Danny looked at him, the older man had his eyes closed.

"How do the cows get through here?" Ethan asked. He'd been full of curiosity and questions about so many things that Danny had been entertained by the ongoing conversation between him and Tom for most of the morning. It helped take her mind off the fact that she couldn't feel her fingers anymore due to her constant grip on the reins.

"They do surprisingly well on steep terrain," Tom answered without turning around. "I've never taken a cow through here, though. I've only ridden it. It's much easier to…or, I should say that it *used* to be easier to simply haul the cattle in a truck.

There's a good chance we'll get to find out exactly how they manage it if we organize a drive with Jesper."

"Cool," Ethan cooed.

"No, not cool," Sam echoed. "Sorry, Tom, you'll have to count me out of that adventure."

Tom chuckled and twisted in his saddle to call back to Sam, "I won't hold it against you!" Tango chose that moment to balk at a particularly large rock in the path.

Danny gasped as she watched Tom's lightning-fast reflexes and expert riding skills save him from a horrible fall. The ground to their right sloped down at a stomach-clenching incline and was littered with large, jagged outcroppings and sparse trees.

"Whoa!" Ethan whooped, as his dad got firmly situated in his saddle again. "Nice recovery. I'll give ya a nine-point-five. Lost half a point for the cursing."

Danny couldn't believe they were joking about it. If that had been Ethan riding Tango…she shook her head, unable to fathom it. While his arm seemed to be doing better than the night before, he still favored it. She was nervous for him, even though he was on the mild-mannered Lily.

As her own horse approached and then carefully stepped around the same rock that nearly unseated Tom, Danny debated dismounting and hiking for a while. She'd already done it once and it didn't really seem to slow them down much. While she wanted to get to Mercy as badly as everyone else, she preferred to be in one piece.

An eagle cried out from somewhere near the ridgeline on their left and another one answered, circling high above. The valley spread out below them was steep and narrow, but she could see a small stream and plenty of dense foliage nestled at the bottom. With the jagged peaks jutting up from all sides, it was the most breathtaking country Danny had ever been in, and she'd done her fair share of hiking in the Rockies.

Tom Miller was in his element. Whether it was due to the safety of the mountains, or his concussion improving, he was much more relaxed and quicker to smile. Perhaps it was a combination of the two, though it really didn't matter why. Danny was just relieved to see his mood improving and the interaction between him and Ethan increasing. It was good that they would have each other to lean on once they got home.

Home. Danny wasn't sure what the word meant to her anymore. In spite of the years she'd lived in Helena, her small apartment near the fire department had never really felt like home. She'd be okay if she never went back. But was Mercy home? Her father's house was a small, one-bedroom cabin. The few times Danny spent the night, she'd slept on the couch. She certainly wasn't going to complain about the accommodations after everything they'd been through, but when thinking about the long-term, and where she belonged? It was hard for Danny to wrap her brain around the concept. Maybe that was why she was feeling more anxious, instead of relieved, as the miles fell behind them on the trail. As hard as the past two weeks had been, she at least had a clear goal and purpose. Part of that was bringing her dad the heart medication she knew he needed, and she was going to fail at even that. Knowing how the lack of medicine would determine her dad's future weighed heavily on Danny.

Grace's barking interrupted Danny's thoughts and she dared to shift in the saddle to seek her out. The retriever wasn't bothered at all by the terrain, and had found a new favorite rodent to chase up any tree she could find. Tom called them marmots, another animal she'd never seen before. About the size of a small beaver, they looked like overgrown guinea pigs. Or maybe more like a prairie dog, Danny hadn't quite decided. Grace was apparently determined to catch one, much to Sam's despair. His horse didn't like barking dogs and every time she picked up another trail, the mare would snort and toss her head. Though she remained sure-footed, Sam was convinced he was going to be thrown off at any moment.

"Grace!" Danny scolded, preempting Sam's pleas. "Come! Get back here, girl. Leave it! Leave the little rat thing alone!"

"It's not a rat," Ethan laughed.

"Close enough," Sam said, holding tightly to the saddle horn.

The trail began to dip down towards the bottom of the valley and Danny got her first good look at the next few miles they'd be traversing. She heard Sam moan from behind her as he saw it, too. It appeared that they would cross at the bottom and then up and *over* the other side.

"Once we get over that ridge," Tom said while pointing at the distant peak, "it's not nearly as steep. That's the point where I normally turned around. I've only been this far one other time."

"How much farther from there to Mercy?" Sam asked.

Tom removed his cowboy hat and scratched at his mop of overgrown black hair. "It's been a couple of years, and I was hunting then, so wasn't really paying attention to the actual time on the trail. I'd guess, so long as we don't get held up by anything, that it shouldn't take more than a couple of days."

"Two days?" Ethan moaned. "I thought it was more like one."

"This stretch is a little longer than I thought it was," Tom admitted. "We'll be lucky to make it out of here before we have to make camp tonight. It might not be a whole two days, Ethan, but I don't want to underestimate it, either. It's not like I've got GPS to guide us."

They were already starting down what looked like the scariest part of the path and Danny tried to focus on the far side of the ravine and the flatter ground Tom promised was on the other side. A small rockslide skittered ahead of them, disrupted by the horses, and the sound of the rocks hitting far below made odd, hollow echoes.

"Uh-uh," Danny said, unable to stomach it any longer. Reining her horse in, she gingerly slung a leg over and dropped precariously to the uneven ground. "I can't do it."

Tom glanced back without comment, but Ethan didn't have a problem giving her a hard time. "Come on, Danny! You're a firefighter. I thought you're supposed to be brave."

"There's a difference between brave and stupid," Danny said without much humor. "Sort of similar to running into a burning building. You only do it if there's a life that needs saving, and it's safe enough to do it. This? I'd compare it to running into an empty, burning building without any bunker gear on."

"An excellent analogy," Sam agreed, also sliding from his horse.

"Besides," Danny added as she started leading the horse, already feeling better with her feet on solid ground. "I don't have anything to prove. I never claimed to be a…horsewoman. Or, whatever it is you call a woman that rides a horse. A cowgirl?"

Ethan laughed.

"Cowgirl is fine," Tom offered, and Danny could tell he was trying not to laugh too.

She didn't mind being their source of entertainment, so long as it meant she didn't have to worry about meeting a rocky demise.

After an hour of constant descent, the ground eventually started to flatten out and trees began to offer more shelter from the sun. It was back in full force after the storm from the day before, and the stream would offer a welcome break.

Danny and Sam were a few minutes behind, so when they finally reached the bottom, they found Tom waiting for them, still on Tango. Ethan had already dismounted and had a fishing pole in the water.

"What's wrong?" Danny asked when she saw the look on Tom's face. She didn't think he would be irritated with them for lagging behind.

Tom pointed without comment to the south, straight down the narrow valley. Danny could see several thin columns of white smoke in the distance. It couldn't be more than a couple of miles away.

"What are you thinking?" Sam asked when he spotted it.

"That we should check it out." Tom dismounted in one smooth motion and did some quick stretches while he spoke. "This close to Mercy, I'd like to know who's up here. There's at least three fires burning, so it's more than a survivor or two."

"You don't think the military would be trying to set up a FEMA camp in a remote area like this?" Danny asked, her heartbeat speeding up at the thought.

"Dillinger knows about Mercy," Sam reminded them. "I wouldn't put it past him."

Tom squinted against the sun and continued to stare at the smoke. "No," he finally said with a shake of his head. "That wouldn't make sense. Even as stupid as Dillinger is, he wouldn't send his men randomly into the mountains. I know a lot of the folks around here who might come into these hills. It's most likely a group of survivors banding together. They might need some help or have useful information."

"I'll go with you," Danny offered. When Sam raised his eyebrows at her, she felt herself getting defensive. "What? It would be dumb for him to go by himself. You and Ethan both need to rest, and you can catch us dinner and filter some water while we're gone."

"She's right," Tom agreed. "We'll leave the horses and Grace," he added, bending down to pet the dog. "Sorry, girl, but we don't want to announce our arrival."

After a brief debate with Ethan about why he couldn't go, Tom and Danny left on foot with only some water and their sidearms. Since Jesper gave them some ammunition, the guns were once again more than just visual deterrents. Tom estimated it wouldn't take more than a half hour or so to reach the other camp and they wanted to move quickly.

"You must be excited about seeing your dad," Tom said after they'd gone a couple hundred feet.

Danny didn't answer right away, deciding it was okay to be honest with him. "I am, but I'm also nervous."

Tom glanced over at her, surprised. "Really? Why would you be nervous?"

"I'm not really sure," she said slowly. "I think it's because I didn't manage to get the beta blockers he needs for his heart." Tom didn't say anything in response, and she was thankful for his silence. "Without the meds, he'll eventually be a walking time bomb just waiting to have another heart attack."

"So, you're scared to be around him because it might mean being there to watch him die," Tom said bluntly.

Danny's steps faltered and she stopped, staring at him. She wasn't sure if she was offended or simply shocked that he saw through her so plainly.

Tom didn't apologize, and instead offered her a crooked grin. "I think we're more alike than you realize." Gesturing at her to keep moving, they fell back into step together. "When my dad got sick, I was devastated," Tom continued. "I saw him frequently, of course, but as the end drew near…I couldn't handle seeing him that way. I wasn't there the day he died and it's something I've regretted ever since."

"Weren't you living at the farm?" Danny asked, unsure of what else to say.

"No. I got married when I was just twenty and got coaxed into moving to Helena."

"Helena?" Danny asked, confused. She assumed he'd always lived at Miller Ranch and couldn't picture the rugged, cowboy-hat-wearing cattleman living in the city.

Tom grinned again and Danny found herself helpless to smile

back. "My wife wanted to go to college and although I loved the farm, I'd also always dreamed of what life outside of Mercy was like. Well, I found out. I worked construction for years, while my wife got a good career in architecture."

Danny didn't know why, but she found it weird to hear Tom talk about his wife. For some reason, she hadn't thought he'd been married. "I guess I had this picture in my head that you always had the perfect family life," Danny admitted. "I was even jealous. I hardly know my mom. She's been an alcoholic my whole life and went to live with her parents in Hawaii after Dad divorced her when I was a teen."

The words were out of her mouth before she even realized it, and Danny almost got her hand up fast enough to stop it. She was left embarrassed and wondering why in the world she just shared a part of herself with Tom that even her closest friends didn't know about.

Tom stopped her with a hand on her arm. When Danny forced herself to look at him, she was relieved to see that he wasn't staring at her with pity but the same ole easygoing expression he always wore. "My mom loved my dad fiercely, and although I didn't appreciate it at the time, I had a great childhood," he said. "It took making my own mistakes to figure out what I had in Mercy, so I didn't hesitate to go back when Mom asked me to. Ethan's mom didn't see things the same way, and that was okay. Our relationship had already been over for a while at that point. My only regret is not being a bigger part of Ethan's life for the past five years."

Danny found herself leaning into his hand. She was coming to understand that Tom was the kind of man whose word you could trust, and he could handle the weight of his friend's problems. And Danny really needed that kind of friend.

A blood-curdling scream cut through the air, startling them both. Jumping, Danny's hand went automatically to her holster, and she saw Tom's do the same. It sounded like it came from the same direction as the smoke. Another scream quickly followed, confirming it wasn't that far away.

Tom raised a finger to his lips and then cautiously crept forward. Danny kept close to him, her heart racing and breath coming in quick gasps. Whatever was happening in that camp, she wasn't sure she wanted to find out.

They moved soundlessly through the dense trees that lined the creek, and after a few hundred more feet, saw the first of the tents. Tom grabbed at Danny's hand and pulled her down behind a large fallen tree. It was likely uprooted the night before during the storm, and there was still fresh mud around it. Ignoring the muck, Danny pushed up against it while peeking through its branches.

"I count six tents," Tom whispered close to her ear. "At least eight men with a couple of rifles, and three fires."

Danny nodded silently. The men she could see definitely weren't military, but she didn't see any women or children, either. There were only two horses tied up on the far side of the clearing they were using, and they were muddy and worn out. All of the men were filthy.

Another scream filled the miserable camp and that was when Danny noticed the man tied to a tree, near the center of it all. A larger man had been standing in front of him, blocking him from their view. As he stepped aside, Danny gasped.

"He isn't gonna tell us anything," someone shouted from the other side of the fire, close to where the prisoner was tied up. "Same as his friend. Just finish it, would ya? I'm tired of listening to his hollerin'."

As he'd been talking, the man gestured toward the horses, and Danny realized that what she'd thought were bags, was actually a body. She assumed the two horses belonged to the prisoner and dead man.

As Danny watched, the larger man revealed the knife he'd been using to administer small cuts to the prisoner's face. Holding the point to the man's right eye, he shouted at him. "If you want to keep your eye, this is your last chance! Where did you get these horses? What's the Pony Express?"

"I already told you, I'm not military! I'm just from our small town—"

"Argh!" the executioner growled in rage, and flipping the knife around, moved it swiftly towards the man's throat.

Danny's brain went on autopilot. Without even thinking, she started to lunge forward, intent on stopping the carnage and saving the poor man's life. Before she could make it over the log, strong arms wrapped her up from behind and hauled her backwards, pinning her to the ground.

It took only a moment for her brain to catch up to her raw emotions, and she knew it was helpless. They were far outnumbered and probably out-armed. Danny stopped struggling against Tom. His eyes, green and intense, were only inches from hers and they begged her to be silent. Fortunately, the scream that had been building in her chest never ripped free, and she instead choked it back with a sob.

Tom's hands moved from her arms to her face, and he pulled her up against his chest as she cried. "What have we become?" she gasped into his shirt, as terrified by the fact that they couldn't do anything to stop it as she was by what they'd seen.

"It's okay," Tom assured her, still holding on with an iron grip. "We'll be in Mercy soon and this will all be over. We can stop running."

"Can we?" she asked. Pulling back, Danny looked into his eyes again, searching for some sort of redemption. "How can we ever be sure of who we are, after everything we've done?"

Danny looked away then, defeated. "I was already running long before the flashpoint ever hit."

CHAPTER 22

CHLOE
Medical Clinic, Mercy, Montana

"I GUESS this means you won't be able to do much do-si-doing at the dance?" Crissy teased, while holding Trevor's hand.

He was propped up on one of the cots that had been set up in the makeshift clinic inside Mercy's combination elementary/high school. Though Trevor's face was banged up and he had several visible scrapes and bruises on his hands and arms, it was his left leg that took the brunt of the fall.

Dr. Olsen used words like "miraculous" and "lucky" to describe the accident scene and how Trevor had escaped with nothing worse than a severely broken leg. Apparently, he'd managed to leap from the opposite side of the wagon as it made its fateful plunge over the edge.

When she and Crissy got to the clinic to see him the night before, he'd been unconscious from all the morphine the doc had shot him up with. Chloe was already irritated at that point, since they'd sped there thinking he was about to die. Then, the storm hit before they could leave and trapped them in the clinic for *hours.*

While Chloe didn't hesitate to return with Crissy that afternoon, she was already testy. Her patience was running short and she really needed to get back to the farm to help with the cleanup from the storm. Sandy and Bishop risked their lives the night before to secure the herd, and several of them still broke through the fence when a tree blew over and took out a section. They'd been out all day trying to round them up, and the rest of the chores weren't getting done.

A coughing fit drew Chloe's attention to a man on a cot across the room. Next to him was a young girl hooked up to IV fluids. She was constantly moaning, and her parents were sitting to either side of her, attempting in vain to console her. Chloe knew that she had what Dr. Olsen suspected was appendicitis. She had overheard a debate between the doctor and her only nurse as to whether they should risk surgery, and their decision to try the antibiotics first. That led to another conversation about how low they were on the medication.

Several other beds were occupied by a mix of elderly and young patients who had run out of various drugs and couldn't function anymore. "Insulin" was a word spoken often, as were "pain medicine", "psych meds", and "steroids". Chloe's greatest takeaway from her visits at the clinic was that she prayed she never got sick. She didn't know how Trevor could stand to volunteer all of his time there. Give her a hungry cow and a dirty horse stall any day.

"I'm afraid Trevor won't be doing much of anything on his feet for at least two weeks," Dr. Olsen said as she approached his bed. "Not even with the help of crutches. Total bedrest until then. I managed to reset the bone, but it should have been surgically pinned back into place. If he moves it too much, it won't heal right."

"You should have seen it!" Trevor exclaimed, his face becoming animated. "The bone was totally sticking up out of the skin. Like, you could *see* the bone!" he emphasized, poking his index finger up and wiggling it like it was his leg bone. "I didn't think bones were literally white like that."

"Ugh," Crissy moaned, pushing his hand back down onto his lap. "Would you *please* stop talking about it? Or I'm seriously going to throw up on you."

"It's too bad you didn't hit your head instead," Chloe joked, poking him in the skull. "There would have been a lot less damage."

Trevor screwed up his nose and made a face at her, but there was a wariness in his eyes that hadn't been there before. Chloe suspected he saw a lot worse than his leg at the accident, and he was partially coping by focusing on his own injures instead.

"Not too much talking," Dr. Olsen cautioned before leaving the three of them alone. "I don't want his asthma stirred up any more than it is. We're running low on inhalers."

Chloe eyed the small blue medication dispenser that sat on the table next to his bed. It scared her to think of what would happen once it ran out. Her stomach clenched. There weren't any labs anywhere producing more medicine, or pharmacies that were open to go buy it from. Once it was gone…

"Don't worry," Crissy was saying playfully, still holding Trevor's hand. "I'll save you a dance for next time."

Trevor smiled and then looked shyly at Crissy. "Promise not to dance with anyone else?"

Chloe saw it then. The way Crissy was holding his hand and how she leaned in closer when Trevor spoke. The naturally flirty girl wasn't just teasing him. At some point, she'd developed real feelings for Trevor, and he obviously felt the same way. It had prob-ably started as just some sort of end-of-the-world infatuation, and then flourished in the closed society that Mercy had turned into.

Chloe sat back, stunned by the revelation, and not really understanding why. She wasn't jealous. She had absolutely no romantic interest in or feelings for Trevor. Chloe really couldn't even fathom how Crissy was interested in the young, often irritating teen.

But clearly, she was. Another round of light giggles punctuated her thoughts and Chloe had to resist the urge to run from the room. They were both her friends. Her *best* friends, so she would figure out a way to deal with it. She looked at their hands again, clasped together, and realized that perhaps it was the closeness she envied.

Over the past week, Chloe had become so absorbed in the work on the farm that she was distancing herself…no, *insulating* herself from everyone around her. It was easier that way. She desperately missed her parents and was afraid of getting too close to anyone else. They all ended up leaving her in the end, anyway.

Mortified she was about to start crying, Chloe tried to think of a way to excuse herself without being obvious, but her brain wasn't cooperating as the intense emotions swelled. Instead, she turned to her old friend, anger. It was such an easier emotion and she slipped gratefully into its dark embrace.

"Didn't three people die yesterday?" Chloe hissed, her eyes narrowing. "I don't think we should be talking about dances and making light of the whole situation."

When Crissy turned to glare at her, the shock on her friend's face was enough to subdue Chloe, and the shame that followed was as familiar to her as the anger.

Embarrassed, Chloe stood and turned away, hoping that no one else had witnessed the exchange. To her dismay, the new pastor, of all people, was standing only two beds away, apparently praying over someone.

He was staring straight at her, and not even trying to be polite and hide the fact that he had overheard the whole thing. She averted her eyes from his and stared at his hands instead, figuring he was holding a Bible or cross, or something equally religious. Instead, it looked like some sort of syringe and he quickly stuffed his hands into the front pocket of his sweatshirt. Wasn't a priest supposed to wear robes?

Chloe looked back up at his face to confirm that it was, in fact, the same Father Rogers they'd been introduced to when they first arrived at the clinic the day before. It had been a chaotic scene and there were a lot of upset people running around, but Chloe never forgot a face.

Especially not his, which was very distinct with his poster-boy jawline, thick blond hair, and striking green eyes. He smiled at her then, one she had no doubt was meant to be disarming. However, there was something about the man that made Chloe's skin crawl, and her eyes narrowed with disdain instead of friendliness.

Her humiliating scene forgotten, Chloe stood frozen by the exchange, and as his smile turned into a sneer, the crawling sensation spread from her stomach and traveled up her spine.

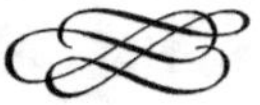

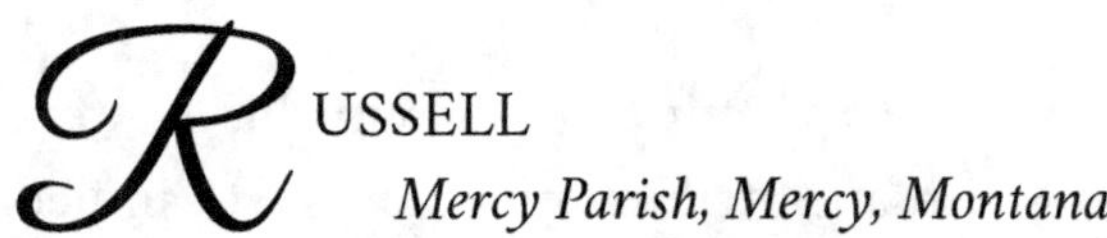

CHAPTER 23

R USSELL
Mercy Parish, Mercy, Montana

RUSSELL WAS EXPECTING the knock at the back door of his church apartment. The timing couldn't have been any better, since he'd just set the tea kettle on top of the woodstove to boil.

Another round of insistent knocking erupted as he casually made his way to the door, whistling under his breath as he went. Everyone was always in a rush, even the old priest. You'd think the end of the world would encourage people to slow down a little and spend more time enjoying the small things. Someone should caution Father White that all that stress was bad for his health.

Grinning, Russell opened the door with a flourish, revealing Father White with his hand raised, ready to knock again. "Father!" Russell gushed, pulling the door open all the way and stepping aside. "Please, come in."

"I can't stay long," the older man grumbled as he ambled inside.

The back door opened into the kitchen and both men took a seat opposite each other at a small wooden table. The woodstove glowed nearby, the wood inside audibly cracking and popping. With a pillar candle burning on the counter, pushing back the shadows as the sun began to set outside, it was a cozy setting. "What brings you by?" Russell asked, clasping his hands in front of him on the table.

"I'm going to get straight to the point and keep this brief," Father White said without any preamble. "While I appreciate your situation and what you've been through, I don't feel you are the right man to help guide the congregation of Mercy." The old priest cleared his throat and shifted on the wooden chair. "You're welcome to stay here in the apartment until you can find proper accommodations, of course."

Russell hung his head in contrition, enjoying the role-playing. "I thank you for your generosity, Father." Looking up, he saw the surprise on the pastor's face and felt a small rush of excitement as his plot unfolded exactly as he'd foreseen it. "I have been doing a lot of soul-searching these past few days that I've been in Mercy and I have to say that I agree with you. I'm not currently in the right frame of mind to conduct the work of God."

"Well, I...um, I'm glad to hear that you've come to the same conclusion." Father White was clearly flustered by the conversation. Apparently, he hadn't prepared the proper speech. "Perhaps with time, you will find your way back to the word of God."

Tilting his head slightly, Russell pursed his lips and then nodded slowly, as if taking the wise words to heart. "Perhaps."

The kettle began to whistle and Russell's head jerked up as if he'd forgotten he had put it on. "Oh! I was about to have some tea, Father. Won't you join me?"

When the priest hesitated, Russell was excited by the extra

challenge, rather than concerned he might leave. "I found a lovely blend in the cupboard, as well as some sugar. And I would appreciate some guidance as to what scripture I should study while dealing with my internal conflict."

The request for mentorship was something Father White couldn't say no to, and as Russell expected, he was flattered by the request. "Certainly, Father Rogers. If you would fetch me a pen and paper, I'd be happy to give you a list."

Minutes later, as the tea steeped and Father White was distracted by his list-making, Russell stood at the counter and added the liquid antihistamine to his cup. He wasn't sure if the berry-flavored medication would be enough to do much, but it would have to do. His options were extremely limited and it was the only liquid sedative he could identify at the clinic in the brief time he'd had.

When the herbal tea was added, it smelled like any other concoction and he figured the priest would write off any odd taste as a cheap brand and lack of cream. He placed the cup silently in front of the other man, as he continued to write, not wanting to interrupt his train of thought.

Ten minutes later, the cup was empty, the sheet of paper was nearly full of scriptures, and Father White was rubbing at his eyes. "My goodness, it's barely past dinner time and I'm afraid I'm already needing a bed."

Russell removed the teacups and carried them to the sink. With his back to the room, he wordlessly took out the preloaded syringe from his sweatshirt pocket and popped off the protective cap.

"It's completely understandable," Russell replied as he turned around. "You're a frail, elderly man who's been sick with radiation poisoning for two weeks. Why, you could drop dead at any moment and no one would think much of it."

As Russell moved up behind him, Father White's hands froze,

pen in hand, when he grasped what the other man had said. "Why would you say—"

Russell moved quickly, jabbing the hypodermic needle into the other man's right shoulder and injecting him with at least a couple of milligrams of morphine before Father White could bat it away with his sluggish reflexes.

"Ouch!" Rubbing at his shoulder and lurching to his feet, the priest knocked his chair over as he clumsily spun around to face his attacker. "What...what in the world are you doing?" He blinked twice, slowly, and then staggered sideways a couple of steps.

Russell dropped the syringe and removed another from his pocket. The subcutaneous injection of morphine was only a means to compound the old man's sedation. He would have preferred to have done it without the extra aid, but it was critical that there be no outward signs of a struggle.

As the potent opioid was slowly absorbed, it combined with the antihistamine, enhancing its effects. The look of confusion on Father White's face turned to anger and then fear. He reached out blindly at the table for support, his legs beginning to buckle. "What are you?" he groaned, looking up at Russell, his eyes wide and pupils pinpoints.

Methodically removing the cap from the new needle, Russell considered the question carefully before answering. Bending over so that his face was close to the priest's, he spoke deliberately, making sure the other man understood him. "The meek shall inherit the earth."

Before Father White could react, Russell slid around behind him. Reaching up with his left hand, he grasped the taller man's forehead, anchoring his elbow against his shoulder to put him in a modified sort of headlock. Pulling his dazed victim back into his chest to brace him, he reached around with the syringe and lined it up precisely with the carotid artery in his neck. Though an extremely efficient way of administering a lethal dose of drugs, it was also quite tricky. Fortunately, he'd spent some time in the past perfecting the technique.

With the needle in place, Russell slowly injected the morphine while using nearly all of his strength to hold the man still. Father White moaned against the pain of the large dose coursing through his body and kicked out with the last throes of life.

"Shhhh," Russell murmured, his mouth against his victim's ear. "Don't fight it. Soon, you'll simply stop breathing and cease to exist."

His mind already moving on to what other steps he had left to complete, Russell waited patiently, staring at the woodstove over the top of Father White's gray head. Once several hours had passed, when it was well past dark, he would carry the priest's body the short distance across the yard and into his house. There, he would arrange him so that when found the next day, it would appear that he'd simply died in his sleep.

The syringe wouldn't leave a noticeable mark and Russell had a bottle of pain pills to place on the nightstand, which should provide the doctor with enough of an excuse for the Father's small pupils. That was, if the pupils remained contracted after death, due to the medication. Russell wasn't sure if they would dilate the way they normally did and it was a curiosity for him. Perhaps he could find a way to be there when the doctor arrived, so he could get the answer firsthand. After all, he was working with the charming doctor now. That was how he'd been able to acquire the morphine.

A gasping sound reminded Russell that he still had more immediate matters to attend to. Releasing Father White from his hold, he supported his limp body and lowered him carefully to the floor. His color already ashen, he was quickly succumbing to the suppression of his central nervous system, with the respiratory drive the first to go.

While Father White lay dying, the final dregs of air being sucked into his lungs with each hard-fought breath, Russell crouched over him. A hand to either side of his body, he leaned in until their cheeks almost touched. "Don't worry, Father. I'll tend to your flock. I have some very special plans for them."

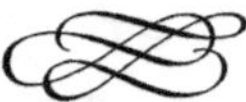

Tom

Lewis & Clark National Forest, near Mercy, Montana

THE CLIMB LEADING up out of the valley had been a somber one. They intentionally waited until the sun started to slip below the ridgeline so they would be in the shadows, and less visible to anyone in the valley who might be looking up. The last thing they needed was for the group of killers to come after them.

Tom glanced over his shoulder, confirming that they were all still moving. He had to admit to being shaken up. Even after all the things they'd been through, the last thing he thought he'd find that deep in the mountains was a man being tortured to death. He understood Danny's reaction and all of the personal intro-spection it brought with it. They were literally in a new world…a sort of purgatory where they had what could be considered an opportunity to start over. To do things better than the first time. Instead, humanity seemed destined to waste the chance at a fresh start and turn barbaric. In some cases, almost primal, where the only thing that mattered was survival, even when that was at the cost of everyone else.

What if they got to Mercy only to discover that it wasn't any different than the other places they'd been over the past two weeks? Tom shook his head. He knew in his heart that Miller Ranch would always be a refuge, no matter what happened in the rest of the world. If Mercy was lost, so be it. He'd make sure that Ethan was safe, and if possible, Danny and Sam, too.

"I don't see anyone following us," Danny said, her voice strained. She hadn't spoken much since running from the spot in the mud where he'd held her down. Tom tried not to think about how he'd felt an overpowering need to protect her. He had his son to worry about, and that was enough.

"I'll still feel a lot better once we're on the other side of that crest," Sam answered. "Do you think we'll be able to get a few more miles between us before it gets too dark? I might be overreacting, but I'm feeling nervous about starting a fire."

Tom forced a smile and twisted in his saddle so he could talk to the older man. "Once we're past this, they won't be able to see a thing from the valley floor," he said, waving a hand at the craggy rocks looming above them. "I didn't see any tracks anywhere along the creek bed, so I figure they came up the valley from the other end. I'm almost certain there's a trail a ways down there that heads east and connects to the freeway. I doubt they even know about this old trail. It's not on any maps."

Sam looked relieved. "Well, why didn't you say that before?"

"It was kinda obvious no one else had been through there," Ethan jested, never missing an opportunity to tease his highly intelligent friend.

"I was more focused on things like not falling to my death," Sam retorted, happy to play along with the mock argument.

Tom glanced back again, comforted by the normal banter,

and found Danny staring at him. "Thank you," she said softly, while Ethan and Sam continued their lively conversation.

That wasn't what Tom expected. "For what?"

Danny looked down at her hands, clearly not used to speaking openly about her feelings. "I don't know if Sam and I would have made it without you."

Tom waited for her to meet his eyes again so that he was sure she would know he was being honest. "Danny, I think you might have that backwards. You guys were doing pretty well before I, um…attacked you one night." He grinned crookedly at her until she smiled back. "And I seem to remember *you* doing most of the saving."

She blushed slightly, but didn't look away. "That's not really what I meant."

Tom paused, not sure if he was interpreting her correctly. He'd never been very good at understanding women. "You know," he said, his smile growing. "I hope you don't think you'll be getting rid of me that easily once we've made it to Mercy. I'm pretty sure I owe you a beer, and you owe me a story."

Laughing, Danny nodded in agreement. "I think you might be right."

Tango chose that moment to scramble up and over the final section of the trail, forcing Tom to turn back. Relief flooded over him as he was finally able to accept that they'd managed to avoid a confrontation with the gang of killers. Although they still had another day or two of hard riding ahead of them.

As he rounded a large protruding boulder and crested the top, Tom got a clear view to the west and the setting sun. His breath catching in his throat, he reined Tango in and sat for a moment, soaking it in.

"Yes!" Ethan hooted as he rode Lily past him at a gallop and made a large circle on the broad, grassy slope. Grace chased after them, barking, picking up on everyone's excitement.

"Is that Mercy?" Sam asked, stopping next to Tom. As the only one in their group to have never seen the town, he had no idea what it looked like.

"I think it is!" Danny cheered, getting down from her horse and walking out onto the grass to get a better view of the valley.

"I thought it'd be bigger," Sam joked as he slowly climbed out of his own saddle.

Tom stared out at the miniature buildings in the distance, located far below them in a wide valley, with two more mountain ranges between them. "It's an old mining town," Tom explained while dismounting. Tango was eager to graze on the lush green grass and it wasn't worth trying to hold him back. "It used to be twice the size, back when the mines were still in operation. When they shut down, it almost turned into another ghost town until my great-grandfather proved how lucrative the land was for cattle."

Ethan, having abandoned Lily to her own grazing, ran back over to where the rest of them were standing. Tom put an arm around his son's shoulders, still shocked at how tall he was getting. Looking up at his dad, Ethan grinned and moved closer. "We did it."

Not trusting himself to speak, Tom turned back to take in the view. If he ignored the clear delineation of dying trees, and the lack of movement on the roads below, he could almost imagine that nothing had changed.

A flash of light in the sky to the north taunted his thoughts, and he stared hard at the boiling clouds on the far horizon. Normally, weather systems didn't come from that direction, but he was learning to expect the unexpected.

Danny moved up on his other side, and without thinking, Tom took ahold of her hand and pointed it toward the mountains on their left, rising up from the west side of Mercy. "There,"

Tom directed, moving her hand up and down. "Close to half of that hillside belongs to the Miller Ranch."

"It's beautiful," Danny breathed. Turning her hand, she intertwined her fingers with his, and Tom squeezed back, holding on tightly. It felt right, as they stood there on the bluff, with so many things still unknown.

Danny draped her other arm over Sam's shoulders, and Grace loped around them all, before settling down in front of Tom. Staring up at him with her gentle brown eyes and lolling tongue, she made it all seem so simple.

Tom looked then at Sam and Danny, and finally Ethan. "You're right," he said, agreeing with his son. "We're going home to Mercy."